Meet the staff of
THE TREEHOUSE TIMES

AMY—The neighborhood newspaper is Amy's most brilliant idea ever—a perfect project for her and her friends, with a perfect office location—the treehouse in Amy's backyard!

ERIN—A great athlete despite her tiny size, Erin will be a natural when it comes to covering any sports-related story in the town of Kirkridge.

LEAH—Tall and thin with long, dark hair and blue eyes, Leah is the artistic-type. She hates drawing attention to herself, but with her fashion-model looks, it's impossible not to.

ROBIN—With her bright red hair, freckles and green eyes, and a loud chirpy voice, nobody can miss Robin—and Robin misses nothing when it comes to getting a good story.

Keep Your Nose in the News with
THE TREEHOUSE TIMES Series
by Page McBrier

(#1)UNDER 12 NOT ALLOWED
(#2) THE KICKBALL CRISIS
(#3) SPAGHETTI BREATH

Coming Soon

(#5) DAPHNE TAKES CHARGE

PAGE McBRIER grew up in Indianapolis, Indiana, and St. Louis, Missouri, in a large family with lots of pets. In college she studied children's theater and later taught drama in California and New York. She currently lives in Rowayton, Connecticut, with her husband, Peter Morrison, a film producer, and their two small sons.

THE TREEHOUSE TIMES
#4

First Course: Trouble

Page McBrier

AN AVON CAMELOT BOOK

THE TREEHOUSE TIMES #4: FIRST COURSE: TROUBLE
is an original publication of Avon Books. This work has
never before appeared in book form.

AVON BOOKS
A division of
The Hearst Corporation
105 Madison Avenue
New York, New York 10016

First Avon Camelot Printing: February 1990

CAMELOT TRADEMARK REG. U.S. PAT. OFF. AND IN OTHER COUNTRIES,
MARCA REGISTRADA, HECHO EN U.S.A.

Printed in the U.S.A.

OPM 10 9 8 7 6 5 4 3 2 1

For Ellen Krieger, with thanks

THE TREEHOUSE TIMES

#4

First Course: Trouble

Chapter One

"Amy! Where did you go?"

Amy Evans wriggled out of the broom closet, being careful not to get her hair or her glasses hooked on anything. "I'm in the kitchen," she shouted.

Amy's best friend, Erin Valdez, appeared in the doorway holding a six-pack of diet soda and a tape deck. "*Now* what are you doing?"

"What do you think?" said Amy, reaching for a giant bottle of Mr. Clean. "We can't have a cleaning party without cleaning stuff!" She grabbed a broom and a roll of paper towels. "Here. Help me."

Erin stuffed some rags under her arm and followed Amy outside toward the treehouse, where their other two friends, Leah Fox and

Robin Ryan, were already supposed to be getting started.

"Look out. Here we come," shouted Erin, waving the rags. "The Kirkridge clean machine!"

Amy laughed at Erin. She was in a really crazy mood today. Maybe she had spring fever.

Now Robin poked her head out the window and stared at Erin. "Oh, good. You're back," she said, ignoring Erin's weird behavior. "We need you to kill all these spiders."

Erin immediately threw everything she was carrying onto the ground. "Spiders, you say? No problem!" She grabbed the broom from Amy. "To the rescue!"

"Eeek." Robin's head disappeared inside.

"Be careful, Erin," Amy shouted. "Don't break anything."

Upstairs, Amy heard Erin yell, "Charge!"

Robin and Leah shrieked.

"Be careful!" Amy said for the second time. She quickly climbed up the ladder and into the main room just as Erin was putting a broom karate chop to one of the spiderwebs.

"Aaay-ee!" said Erin.

Leah ducked down. "Watch it, Erin! I don't want spiders flying onto me."

"Me neither," said Robin. "I hate spiders."

Erin grinned at Amy and then spun the broom toward another corner. "Zap, zap," she said, pulling down another two webs. Today was the official reopening of the tree-house, headquarters of the *Treehouse Times,* a neighborhood newspaper which been started by Amy, Leah, Erin, and Robin after Amy's sixth grade class had toured the offices of the real paper, the *St. Louis Post-Dispatch.* Kirkridge was a suburb of St. Louis, and all winter the girls had met in Amy's kitchen because the treehouse was too cold.

"Prepare to die, spiders," yelled Erin, attacking the next web.

"I think that's enough, Erin," said Robin, dodging Erin's broom. "I'm sure they're all dead by now." Already, the treehouse was starting to look like its old self again. Everything had been uncovered and put back where it belonged. Against one wall sat their old wood-frame sofa, which had been donated by Leah's parents. Opposite that was their card table, which had held a typewriter and their office supplies. Even their soda cooler, which doubled as an end table, was back in its spot next to the sofa. Amy dumped the sodas into the cooler and watched as Robin turned on a Melody Rollins tape and hopped onto the sofa. "Be my all to me," Robin sang as she dusted off the back of the sofa. "Be my all, my only."

"Hey, Robin," said Erin. "Don't break the sofa."

"Ha, ha. Very funny," she said. She did a few fancy turns and then jumped with a thud back onto the floor. "What next?" she asked. Robin had red hair and freckles and was a tiny bit plump. She was still the best dancer of the four, though, probably because she had two sisters in high school who were always making her dance with them.

"Uh, I guess we should dust the card table and chair before we go get the typewriter," said Amy.

Robin nodded and turned up the volume. The rest of them joined in on the song, even Amy, who usually didn't sing aloud for anything, including the "Star Spangled Banner." Maybe they *all* had spring fever.

They danced and cleaned for a long time until the tape finally ended. Then Erin put two fingers in her mouth and whistled loudly. "Hear ye, hear ye. Time to get the typewriter!"

"The typewriter!" echoed Robin.

Erin was sort of a tomboy. She'd been Amy's best friend ever since she'd moved to Kirkridge from California in the third grade. Even though she and Amy were best friends, they didn't look anything alike. Erin was petite, with short dark hair and dark eyes. Amy was average size, with in-between length blonde hair, green eyes, and glasses.

Amy made sure Erin was right about everything being clean and then said, "Let's go!" The typewriter was the most important piece of equipment the newspaper owned. It had belonged to Amy's mother in college, and now Amy used it to type up all the copy for the newspaper. Maybe someday they'd own a computer, but for now the typewriter was perfect. Each month after the paper was typed, Leah, who was the art director, did the layout. Then Amy gave the finished paper to her father, who ran off enough copies for everyone in the neighborhood at his office.

Erin ran to the hatch. "I'll get it."

"Wait," said Amy. "We have to get the office supplies, too, remember?" All of the newspaper's "valuables" were stacked carefully in a corner of the kitchen.

Robin followed them down the ladder. "What about snacks for the cooler?"

"And our art supplies," said Leah, coming too.

Amy laughed. "May as well do the whole thing in one trip."

Inside Amy's kitchen, the girls carefully packed up the typewriter and all the other valuables. When they were all finished,

Robin stuffed a bag of butterscotch balls in one pocket and a pack of bubble gum in the other. "Okay, I'm ready."

In no time, they were back in the tree-house, putting everything back where it belonged.

"Know what I think?" said Leah, looking around. Leah had long dark hair and a skinny body. She also had artistic taste, although sometimes it got a little weird. "This office could stand some redecorating."

Amy surveyed the room. "Like what?" she said cautiously.

"Like the couch should be against *that* wall," she pointed, "and the desk should be against *that* wall. It'll make the room seem larger."

Erin and Amy looked at each other. "She's right," said Erin, jumping forward. "Let's try it." She grabbed one side of the card table.

"I'll do that," said Robin, pushing Erin out of the way.

"I was here first," said Erin, elbowing her way back. "I don't need any help."

Robin picked up the other side of the table anyway and together they started to scoot it across the room.

"Careful, guys," said Amy. "The legs on that thing aren't too steady."

"It's okay," said Erin. "We're almost there."

6

Amy looked down. "Watch out!" she yelled. One of the legs on the table started to fold under.

"There goes the typewriter!" screamed Leah. "Catch it!"

Amy lunged forward. *"Ooomph!"*

With a loud crash, it smashed to the ground.

"Oh no!" said Amy.

Sheets of white paper, scissors, glue, and tape went skidding across the room. In the middle of everything, on its side, lay the typewriter.

For a minute, no one said anything. Then Amy grabbed a sheet of paper, righted the typewriter, and tried to type something.

"Is it okay?" asked Erin.

Amy shook her head. "The keys are stuck," she said. "I can't even get it to type one word."

"Now what do we do?" said Robin. "We can't have a newspaper without a type-writer."

They all stared helplessly at the floor.

"How can I help you girls?"

Amy, Leah, Robin, and Erin stood crowded together inside Schlott's Repair Shop. Amy carefully lowered the typewriter onto the counter. "Can you fix this?" she asked Mr. Schlott.

Mr. Schlott peered through his wire-frame glasses. "What happened to it?"

"It got dropped," said Robin. "Accidentally."

Mr. Schlott shook his head back and forth and bent down over the machine. "Uh huh, uh huh," he muttered, moving his grimy fingers around inside. He pulled his hand out of the machine and wiped his fingers on his apron. "Won't be cheap," he said.

Erin leaned forward. "How much?"

Mr. Schlott looked down again and studied the typewriter. "Forty-seven fifty," he said finally.

"Forty-seven dollars and fifty cents?" gasped Robin.

Mr. Schlott pursed his lips together and shook his head again. "Lot of damage here."

Amy pulled on Erin's arm. "How much do we have in our savings?" she whispered. Erin was the paper's business manager.

"Thirty-three twenty-five," Erin whispered back. "That means we're short"—she quickly added it up in her head—"fourteen twenty-five."

Amy's heart sank. Where would they get the rest of the money?

"I'm not carrying that thing back," said Robin bluntly. "If we're short, we'll have to figure out another way to get the money."

8

"Like what?" said Leah.

Robin thought for a minute. "Like . . . we'll get a loan! I'll ask my dad."

Erin frowned. "What good will that do? We'll still have to pay him back. Besides, I don't like the idea of borrowing from our parents."

"Me neither," said Amy. "It makes us seem like we can't handle things."

Erin turned to Amy. "When's our next edition supposed to come out?"

"Next Friday," said Amy, sighing.

Robin said to Mr. Schlott, "When can we have the typewriter?"

Mr. Schlott slowly stroked his chin. "Next week sometime."

Amy said, "Can we have it by Wednesday? That should give me enough time to type up all the stories." Right now Amy used the two-finger typing technique so she wasn't too fast. She was planning to take typing in summer school this year.

"I'll try," he said.

For the second time, Erin leaned over and whispered into Amy's ear. "But, Amy, *where* are we going to get the money?"

"Erin," said Amy firmly, "don't worry. We'll figure something out. We have to. We can't do the newspaper without the typewriter."

* * *

9

On the way back to the treehouse, the girls had a big fight. It started when Erin said, "I still don't see how we're going to find the money for this."

"Stop worrying, would you?" said Robin. "We'll have a bake sale. We'll have a car wash."

"A bake sale isn't going to earn us fifteen dollars," said Erin. "Not after we pay for the stuff we need to bake, anyway."

"So we'll wash some cars," said Robin.

Erin glared at Robin. "It's not that easy, Robin. Do you know how many cars we'd have to wash to make that much money?"

"What about a raffle?" said Leah. "We could raffle something."

"What?" asked Amy.

Leah shrugged.

Erin said, "None of this would have happened if Robin hadn't tried to help me move the card table."

Robin's neck jutted out. "Don't blame it on *me*," she said. "I was only trying to help."

"I never asked for your help," said Erin. "You just barged in as usual."

"I was following Amy's orders," said Robin.

Amy stared at her. "I didn't give any orders."

"Yes, you did," said Robin.

Leah waved her arms. "Hold it. Hold it. All this fighting isn't doing any good. Besides, it was *me* who said we should move the table."

"And it wasn't anybody's fault," added Amy. "The leg collapsed."

Robin and Erin shut up.

Amy said, "Maybe there's some way the *paper* can earn the money."

They all thought about it. "Wait," said Erin. "I know. We can try and get another advertiser." One of Erin's jobs as business manager was to be in charge of advertising. Each month the Sugar Bowl and the Copy Corner paid to run ads in the paper, and that money was used to cover the paper's expenses, things like glue, scotch tape, and typewriter ribbons. This way the paper could be given away free.

"We have enough space," said Leah, who did the layouts. "Will that be enough money?"

"It will if we can get them to pay for a few months in advance," said Erin. "Besides, it'd be good to have the extra money in the future in case of other emergencies."

"That's a great idea!" said Amy, feeling better already. "Who should we ask? Who really likes the paper?"

"Mr. P. does," said Robin. Mr. Petropoulus owned Aegean Pizza. He sponsored the girls' kickball team, the Treehouse Terrors, which was why they'd never asked him to be an advertiser before.

"Perfect!" said Amy. "I bet he'd love to." Amy didn't know why she hadn't thought of all this herself. It seemed like the perfect solution.

"Let's go right now," said Robin, turning back toward Lincoln Boulevard.

"Do you think he's there?" asked Leah.

"Of course he's there," said Robin. "Mr. P. is always there."

Only he wasn't. When the girls reached Aegean Pizza, the door was locked shut and there was a sign inside the door. ON VACATION. SEE YOU NEXT MONTH.

"Next month!" shouted Robin.

Amy hit her hand against her head. "How could I forget?" she said. "He told me last week that he was going back to Greece to see his family."

"*Now* what?" said Erin.

"Would you stop saying that?" said Amy. "What's with you?" Erin didn't usually worry. Maybe being business manager was starting to be too much for her.

Amy looked up and down the block. "We'll go door to door and ask," she said confidently. "Leah and Robin, you take one side. We'll take the other." She glanced at the clock inside the pizza parlor. Five-fifteen.

"It's too late to start today. We'll go tomorrow after school, okay?"

Erin laughed uneasily.

"What's wrong?" said Amy.

"You weren't with me the first time I tried to get advertisers."

"That was before we were famous," said Robin.

Amy nodded her head in agreement. "That's right," she said. "Everybody knows us now." She grinned. "I bet we get an ad from the first place we ask."

"I hope you're right, Amy," said Erin, shaking her head. "I hope you're right."

Chapter Two

Amy and Erin stood staring at the fancy sign on the large wooden door. ONDINE'S RESTAURANT. JACKET AND TIE REQUIRED. Amy gave Erin a nudge. "Open the door," she whispered.

"No, *you*," Erin whispered back.

Amy looked at Erin. "I've asked at the last five places. Besides, you're the business manager."

Erin didn't budge. "You're the editor. You're the one who said everyone would *love* to advertise in the paper."

Amy winced. "It's not that they wouldn't love to," she said. "Every single person we asked said they liked the paper. It's just that it adds up every month." She paused. "Maybe we should lower the cost."

"Can't," said Erin. "We need every penny to get the typewriter back, remember?"

Amy stared at the sign again. This was their last chance. Every other place they'd asked had said no. Leah and Robin hadn't had any luck, either. "Do you think we should have dressed up?"

"We're not here for dinner," Erin answered. "Besides, it's only four-thirty. They're not open yet."

Amy took a deep breath. "Okay," she said, swinging the heavy door back. "Here we go again."

Inside, Ondine's was almost pitch-dark. Amy had only been here briefly once before, a few months ago right after the restaurant had opened, when she was covering a story and needed to ask the maître d' something.

Now Amy carefully cleared her throat and walked back up to the same podium where the same man wearing a suit and bow tie was bent over a large book. "Excuse me," she said.

The man leaned over. "Yes?"

"I'd like to speak to the owner, please."

The man looked very closely at Amy and then at Erin. Amy wished she'd remembered to brush her hair. "Whom shall I say is here?"

"Amy Evans and Erin Valdez from the

16

Treehouse Times," said Amy for the millionth time that day.

Erin added, "It's a neighborhood newspaper."

"I see," said the man. "One moment, please."

Now that Amy's eyes were adjusted, she took a peek inside the dining room. The walls were covered with mirrors, and in the corner a man was getting ready to play the piano. Every table had a small vase of flowers, a candle in a fancy holder, and a stiff pink tablecloth with matching pink napkins.

"Wow," said Erin, studying the menu. "Look how much they charge for one little brownie. They must make a fortune."

Amy nodded. "Maybe that means they'll buy an ad."

"Maybe," said Erin. She gazed around the room. "I bet even the bathroom is nice. I bet it has little round soaps and a bottle of hand lotion on the sink."

"Probably," said Amy.

A large man wearing a white apron and chef's hat walked up to them. "May I help you girls?" he said. "I am Etienne Choux, owner of Ondine's." His head gave a slight nod.

"And I am Amy Evans and this is Erin Valdez," said Amy, nodding back. "We have a neighborhood newspaper called the *Tree-*

17

house Times. We were wondering if you'd be interested in placing an ad."

The man smiled. "Perhaps."

Amy brightened up. A "perhaps" was a good sign.

"This is a copy of our paper," said Erin, shoving their latest edition under his nose a little too enthusiastically.

"Ah! I have seen this newspaper before!" said Mr. Choux. "So you are the publishers!" His eye skimmed the headline. " 'Trash Bash Set for Saturday'?" he said. "What is a trash bash?"

"It's when everyone pitches in to clean up the neighborhood," said Amy. "It happens every spring."

Mr. Choux smiled. "Oh, I get it. You bash the trash!" Under his breath he added, "Americans!"

Mr. Choux carefully studied the issue. He looked at Erin's "Neighbor of the Month" profile, Robin's gossip column, an editorial by Amy on how important it was for everyone to help keep the neighborhood clean, and a feature story on Midnight, a neighborhood cat who recently had kittens. "Very nice," he said, flipping to the back page. "When I was a boy in Paree, my friend Pierre and I had a little paper too. It was about pets."

Amy smiled politely.

"Who else advertises in here?"

Eric cleared her throat and said, "Until now, it was just the Copy Corner and the Sugar Bowl. We need another customer to help cover our costs." To Amy's relief, she didn't mention that this was their last hope.

Mr. Choux pulled on his beard. "Mmmmm. I see. How much?"

Erin told him the cost. "Only five dollars a month," said Erin. "And we ask you to pay the first three months in advance."

"*Everyone* reads us," Amy chimed in. "We're famous."

Mr. Choux picked up the paper again and flipped through it.

"What do you think?" asked Erin.

"Okay," he said. "I'll do it."

"You *will?*" said Amy incredulously.

"On one condition. You must send someone in to review me."

Amy said, "You mean, do a review of the restaurant?"

"That's right," said Mr. Choux. "I am new in Kirkridge, so I'd like to get the word out that we have fine French cuisine here at Ondine's."

"We'd love to," said Amy, trying to control her excitement. "I'm sure the food here is delicious." She left out expensive.

Chef Choux beamed. "Then it's settled. Show me where you will place my ad."

Erin pointed to the top right corner of the back page. "Our art director will make it up. Her name is Leah Fox. She did the other ads. She's really good."

"Verrry nice," said Mr. Choux. He laughed out loud, a big guffaw that reminded Amy of Santa Claus. "Would you like me to pay for my ad now?"

Erin said, "Not until you approve it."

Mr. Choux nodded. "As you wish. Now when would you girls like to come for dinner? Bring your paar-ents."

"We'll have to let you know," Amy said. "Thank you so much for buying this ad." She was still in shock. "You don't know how much we appreciate it."

"You really don't," echoed Erin.

"My *plaisir*, mesdemoiselles," said Mr. Choux. He smiled and then shook each of their hands. "Now if you will excuse me, I must get back to my pastries."

"Bye, Mr. Choux," said Erin.

As soon as Mr. Choux was out of earshot, Amy squeezed Erin's elbow. "We did it!" she said. "I told you they could afford it."

Erin nodded up and down. "I don't believe it. He hardly even thought about it."

"Let's go find Robin and Leah," said Amy. They walked back out onto Lincoln Boulevard, and Amy squinted.

"There they are," said Erin, pointing to

Robin and Leah who were waiting on the curb across the street. "You guys." She waved her arms back and forth.

"Did you do it?" Robin called.

"Success!" shouted Amy.

Robin and Leah ran back across the street. "That's great," said Robin. "You were in there forever. I was starting to get worried. What was Ondine's like?"

"Expensive," said Erin. "The owner, Mr. Choux, said we should bring our paar-ents when we do our review."

"What review?" asked Leah.

Amy explained how Mr. Choux had asked that they review his restaurant in exchange for buying advertising.

"Is that allowed?" asked Leah.

"Sure," said Amy. "We're doing him a favor and he's doing us a favor."

"So does this mean we get a free meal?" asked Robin.

"Hardly," said Amy. "If Mr. Choux paid for the dinner then we might feel obligated to write only nice things." She looked at the others. "Okay, which one of you wants to write the review? Who knows about food?" Immediately she was sorry she asked because Leah and Erin both pointed to Robin and started to laugh.

"Cut it out, guys," said Robin.

"Wait a second," said Amy. She stared at Leah.

"Why are you staring at *me?*" asked Leah.

"Because you're the perfect person to review the restaurant," said Amy. "You eat out all the time."

"And you can afford it," added Robin.

Leah didn't say anything but they all knew it was true. Leah was an only child, and both her parents had glamorous jobs. Her mother was a buyer for Saks Fifth Avenue and her father had an advertising agency.

Leah didn't seem too happy about Amy's idea. "I don't like to write," she said. "I'm supposed to be the art director, remember?" All Leah cared about was art. She even went to a private school called the Day School, which specialized in art and music.

"I'll help you with the writing if you want," said Amy. "Besides, what's important is what you think of the restaurant."

Leah thought about what Amy had said. "What if I don't like it?" she asked.

"Don't worry, you will," said Amy. "Anyway, it's supposed to be your honest opinion."

Leah didn't say anything.

"Come on, Leah," Erin coaxed. "You're the only one who can read the menu. The only thing I recognized was brownies."

"Well . . ." said Leah. "I guess I could do

it. Andre and Celeste *did* say they wanted to try Ondine's out." Leah always referred to her parents by their first names.

"Great!" said Amy. "We'll put it in this next issue."

The girls reached Amy's driveway and headed toward the treehouse. All of a sudden a horrible yelping noise pierced the air. "What is *that?*" said Amy, turning around.

Robin rushed back to the corner. "Look!" she pointed. "It's a dogfight over near the Sondras'."

"Who is it?" asked Amy, hurrying to her side.

"I can't tell," said Robin. "It's just a lot of fur."

There was another loud yelp. Leah winced.

"Uh oh," said Robin. "I think I see blood."

"Do you see any adults?" asked Amy.

"No," said Robin.

"Me neither," said Amy. She ran over to her garage where she grabbed an old bucket and filled it with water. "Come on," she called. "Let's try and break it up."

In a second, Robin, Erin, and Leah were all rushing toward the scene of the fight. Amy's neighbor, the disgusting Roddy Casper, was already there, trying to stop the dogs by throwing rocks at them.

"Stand back," said Amy. With one big

whoosh, she tossed the bucket of water onto the dogs. They both ran off yelping.

"Do you think they're all right?" asked Erin.

"I hope so," said Amy. "Who do you think they belong to?"

"One of them looked like Hefty," said Robin. Hefty was a black Labrador retriever who belonged to the Kresges, who lived next door to the Sondras.

At that moment Mr. Sondra stuck his head out the door. "Was that Hefty?" he asked.

"I think so," said Amy. Hefty didn't usually fight.

Mr. Sondra shook his head. "Darn dogs. Why aren't they on leashes?"

Amy shrugged. Even though it was against city laws for dogs to be unleashed, Hefty had always roamed. No one in the neighborhood seemed to mind. He was one of those dogs who made himself at home in everyone else's backyard.

Mr. Sondra walked back inside his house, slamming the door.

"I guess he doesn't like Hefty," said Robin.

"I guess not," said Amy. She glanced at the spot where the two dogs had been fighting and was glad she didn't see any blood.

A few minutes later, Amy was surprised to see a police car slowly cruising up the street.

It stopped in front of where they were all still standing.

"Uh oh," said Roddy. "Cops."

A policewoman rolled down her window. "Hi there," she said in a friendly voice. "Someone told us there was a dogfight going on here."

"There was but they ran off," said Robin. She pointed to Amy. "She threw a bucket of water at them."

At that moment, Mr. Sondra burst out of his house and stalked angrily down his front walk. "Isn't there anything you can do about that dog?" he asked the policewoman. "He's a terrible nuisance."

"You can file a complaint," said the policewoman.

"Good," said Mr. Sondra.

Erin rolled her eyes at Amy, and Amy knew just what she was thinking. Hefty was usually pretty good. It was Mr. Sondra who seemed to be getting crankier.

The Sondras were one of the families who had lived in Kirkridge ever since it had been built back in the 1930s. Even their children had children.

The Sondras were famous for their garden, which featured different colors different parts of the year. Right now it was purple.

Mr. Sondra gave all the information to the policewoman. After she left, Robin said, "I wonder if the Kresges are going to get into trouble?"

"I don't know," said Amy, watching Mr. Sondra head back to his house. "Maybe we should keep our ears open."

"Why?" asked Leah.

"Because," said Amy. "You never know. A good story may be developing."

Chapter Three

"Well, what do you think?" asked Leah.

Amy was bent over the card table in the treehouse, carefully studying the ad that Leah had worked up for Ondine's. "I'm not sure I understand this drawing."

Leah peered over her shoulder. "Those are escargots," she explained.

"What?" said Amy.

"Snails," said Leah. "French restaurants serve them all the time."

Amy covered her mouth with her hand so she wouldn't throw up.

"They're delicious," Leah said. "They taste very garlicky."

"No offense, Leah," said Amy, her hand still covering her mouth, "but the only per-

27

son I think they're going to look good to is you."

Leah looked insulted. "Millions of people eat them," she said. "They're a delicacy."

"What about using Ondine's logo instead?" Amy suggested. "Or some nice flowers?" You never knew with Leah.

Leah shook her head. "My art teacher, Ms. Slater, said that art needs to make a statement."

Amy stared at the ad again. "Oh. Well . . ."

"Big news! Big news!" interrupted Robin, popping her head through the opening in the treehouse floor. "Danielle Stevens said she just saw Ms. Underwood kiss Mr. Eric." Mr. Eric and Ms. Underwood were two of the girls' teachers at Kirkridge Middle School.

"Where?" asked Amy.

"On the lips," said Robin.

Amy giggled. "I meant where *were* they? Not where did they kiss!"

"Ohhh!" said Robin. "I get it! The parking lot at school. Danielle swore on a stack of Bibles that they kissed *on the lips.*"

"Maybe they're in love," said Leah.

"Impossible," said Robin. "Ms. Underwood is engaged."

"Then maybe they're friends," said Leah. "Friends sometimes kiss on the lips."

Robin laughed uncomfortably. "Not me."

"Me neither," said Amy. "The only thing

I ever kiss on the lips is my stuffed animals every night before I go to bed." Robin and Leah looked at her like she was weird.

Leah said to Robin, "Why don't you just ask Mr. Eric why he kissed Ms. Underwood?"

"What if he gets embarrassed?" said Robin.

"He can't be that embarrassed," said Amy. "He was in the parking lot."

"I bet they're in love," said Robin. "I bet Ms. Underwood is going to break off her engagement and marry Mr. Eric instead."

"Robin!" said Amy. "You should be careful what you say!"

Robin didn't seem to be listening.

Leah said, "Getting back to this ad . . . if you think it looks okay I'll take it with me tonight."

Robin pointed to Leah's drawing. "What are those things? Snails?"

Leah gave Amy a knowing look. "See?"

"Okay, okay," said Amy. "Tell Mr. Choux I'll stop by tomorrow after school to pick up his check. That way I can get the typewriter on my way home."

Leah grinned and slid the drawing back into her backpack.

Amy said to Robin, "Leah's going to Ondine's tonight."

"Lucky," said Robin.

Leah only shrugged. "No guarantees. I'm not a writer like you guys."

"You're a gourmet, though," said Amy. "That's what counts."

Robin popped open a can of diet soda and said, "It's easy, Leah. All you have to do is order lots of different things, taste them all, and write down what you think. Oh, and be sure not to wear anything tight."

Amy laughed and pulled a copy of the real paper, the *St. Louis Post-Dispatch*, out from under the card table. "Here," she said, flipping to the restaurant review in the food section. "This review is by Roberta Rall. She's the regular food critic. I heard she's pretty picky, but this'll give you a good idea of how they're written."

"How do *you* know she's picky?" Robin asked.

"Vicky told me. They're friends. Sometimes she takes Vicky to eat with her."

"Lucky," said Robin. Vicky Lamb was a reporter for the *Post-Dispatch*. She also happened to live in Kirkridge and was the advisor for the *Treehouse Times*. They all knew her pretty well, especially Amy.

Amy pointed to the review. "See all the things she rates? Food, service, atmosphere, prices . . ."

Robin read part of the review over Amy's

shoulder. " 'Try the chocolate mousse. It's heavenly.' " She sighed.

Amy went on. "Be sure to take lots of notes. You wouldn't believe how much you forget if you don't write it down."

"Good advice," said Robin. "Take as many notes as you can." She looked at the Mickey Mouse clock on the wall. "Don't you need to get ready, Leah?"

"Not really. Our reservation is for eight."

"On a school night?" said Robin.

"We always eat at eight," said Leah. "I guess I *should* get going, though. I have to finish my homework before we leave." She turned to Amy. "Do you want me to call you later?"

"Not unless you want to," said Amy.

Leah nodded. "Okay, then, guys. Wish me luck."

"Good luck," said Robin. "Have fun eating!"

That night Amy was awakened by a terrible noise. She had been dreaming that a friend of hers from school, Katherine Wolf, had just had all her teeth pulled out because something she had eaten made them rot to death, when the noise woke her up. It sounded like something metal crashing.

Amy ran to the window and pressed her nose against the screen. Half the garbage cans on Washington Street had been knocked over, and there was garbage all over the place.

"Yuck," said Amy. "Disgusting." She tried to see who was making the mess. Washington Street didn't have any raccoons, but it did have cats and dogs. Down the block, she heard another garbage can lid clank onto the street. A porch light went on. She heard someone shout, "Hey! Get out of there!" After that it became quiet again. Amy waited a while longer but when nothing more happened she crawled back into bed and fell asleep again.

The next morning when Amy walked down to the bus stop, she realized that the mess was even bigger than she had thought. Whoever was in the garbage cans the night before had really gone to town. Soggy pieces of paper, coffee grounds, eggshells, and melon rinds were strewn from one end of Washington Street to the other.

"Hey, Evans," yelled Roddy from the bus stop. "Your lunch is ready."

"Very funny," Amy said, picking her way through some chicken bones and a pizza crust.

Erin said, "Have you ever seen anything as disgusting?"

"Who do you think did this?" Amy said.

Grant Taylor, Roddy's best friend, said, "I

know! I know! Killer squirrels!" He and Roddy fell to the ground laughing.

Robin came racing up the street. "You guys!" she shouted. "Mr. Sondra and Mr. Kresge are having a big fight."

"Let's go watch," said Roddy. He and Grant took off toward the Sondras'.

"You're going to miss the bus," yelled Erin after them.

"Who cares?" Roddy shouted.

"What are they fighting about?" asked Amy, staring in the direction of the fight.

Robin tried to get her breath back. "Hefty," said Robin. "Mr. Sondra said Hefty was the one who knocked over all the cans."

"Are you sure?" asked Amy. "They were never knocked over before."

"He said he saw him doing it," Robin said.

"That's weird," said Amy. "What did Mr. Kresge say?"

"He called him a lying fool." She started to giggle.

"Are they actually punching each other?" Erin asked. Amy tried to picture the two of them slugging it out.

"No. Just yelling. They're both really mad."

Amy surveyed the street. "I would be too." She saw the bus turn the corner and head up the street.

33

Robin cupped her hands together and shouted, "Bus!"

Roddy and Grant turned around and raced back.

"What a great fight!" said Roddy, climbing the steps into the bus.

"Yeah!" said Grant. "Too bad you guys missed it. Mr. Sondra said Mr. Kresge was a thieving coward, and Mr. Kresge's face turned purple he got so mad."

Amy looked out the bus window at all the garbage. "Did you talk to Mr. Sondra yet?" she asked Robin.

"Not yet," Robin answered.

"I think you should," said Amy. "And Mr. Kresge too. It looks like we may have the start of an interesting story."

On her way home from school that afternoon, Amy stopped by Ondine's to pick up their check. This time she wasn't as nervous talking to the man standing behind the podium. "Hi," she said cheerfully. "May I speak to Mr. Choux, please?"

"One moment," he muttered.

Amy tapped her foot on the carpet and listened to two of the waiters complaining about a customer. "She never tips," said one. "Next time, I'm going to say something."

"Don't do that," said the other one. "Just

add the tip on to her check. That's what I do."

"I'd like to spill an espresso on her lap," said the first.

Mr. Choux came plowing through the tables. "Ahh, Amy!" he said, holding out both his hands. "Your friend was here last evening with her paar-ents. Lovely people. Lovely. I gave them a superb meal."

"Great!" said Amy.

Mr. Choux kissed his fingers. "Swordfish grilled to perfection. Filet mignon, nice and tender."

"Sounds good," said Amy, thinking about the frozen burritos her mother had tossed in the microwave. "What about the ad? Did you like it?"

"Marvelous," he said. "What a talent that girl is. I particularly loved the tiny escargots. Very clever."

Amy smiled.

"Would you like a brownie?" Mr. Choux asked. "Just baked."

"Uh, thanks," said Amy, "but I really should be going. I just came for the money for the ad."

"Ah, right," said Mr. Choux. He fished into his pocket. "Mademoiselle."

"Thanks," said Amy.

Mr. Choux called back to the kitchen, "Jacques, bring me a brownie, would you?"

He winked at Amy. "I'll give it to you to go. Now when do I have the *plaisir* of seeing my ad?"

"The paper comes out this weekend," said Amy, "so you'll see your ad *and* your review."

"Beautiful!" said Mr. Choux. He leaned over one of the tables to pluck a dead flower stem from a vase. "I am so happy we can work out this arrangement."

"Me too," said Amy, getting up to go. "I can't wait to see what Leah wrote."

Jacques came out and handed a wrapped brownie to Mr. Choux, who handed it to Amy. "I look forward to it," he said.

By the time Amy picked up the typewriter and got home, it was pretty late. She was on her way into her kitchen with the typewriter when she heard Leah calling to her from the treehouse.

"Hi," Amy called back. "Can you help me with this typewriter?"

Leah stuck her head out the window. She looked pretty distressed. "Not right now," she said. "I need to talk to you."

Amy set the typewriter on the kitchen steps. "What's wrong?" she asked, hurrying up the ladder.

Leah was sitting in the middle of the treehouse floor, taking swigs from a giant bottle of mineral water. "Bad indigestion," she said and then added, "it's from last night."

"Uh oh," Amy said. "What happened?"

Leah picked up a sheet of notebook paper. "I think I'd better read you my review." She began. " 'If there's one restaurant everyone should avoid, it's Ondine's on Lincoln Boulevard.' " She looked up. "Want to hear the rest?"

"Uh oh," said Amy.

Leah went on. " 'First, let me say that the atmosphere gets a ten. Everything was very beautiful and clean and the ladies' room even had hand lotion. Our waiter's name was Philippe, and he was good, too, except for his English. The food, though, was really bad. It was so bad it gave me indigestion, and my father had to take an Alka-Seltzer when he got home.' "

"He did?" interrupted Amy.

Leah kept reading. " 'The first thing I tried was the pâté, which we all agreed was too dry. After that my mother had the shrimp cocktail. Three measly shrimp was all she got, and they tasted like they'd been soaking in ice water all day. For my entrée I had filet mignon which I asked for medium and I got well done. This was strange because my mother had swordfish that was practically raw. Also, it was supposed to be served with a sauce that never came. Maybe Philippe didn't understand the word for sauce.' "

Amy winced. "Was there anything you liked?" she interrupted.

Leah skimmed the article with her eyes. "Uhhh . . . yes! 'The brownie was delicious but overpriced.' "

Amy groaned.

Leah took another swig of her mineral water. "You said you wanted my honest opinion, right? What did you expect?"

"I expected you'd like it," said Amy. "When I saw Mr. Choux he told me you had a very good meal."

Leah gave a long but polite burp. "Does that answer your question?"

Amy nervously tapped her finger against her glasses. "Stay there," she said. "I'll be right back."

"Where are you going?" asked Leah.

"I think we should talk to Robin and Erin about this."

"Do we have to?" asked Leah.

"They should know what's going on," said Amy. She quickly climbed down the ladder and hurried into her kitchen to use the phone.

Ten minutes later, all four girls were assembled in the treehouse. Amy started things off by saying, "We have something to discuss."

"We know, we know," said Robin. "Somebody's been getting into the garbage and making a mess."

Leah coughed.

"Actually, I had something else in mind," said Amy. "Last night Leah went to try out Ondine's."

"Great!" said Erin. "How'd you like it?"

"I didn't," said Leah.

Erin gulped. "You didn't?"

Robin jumped up from the sofa. "You're *kidding!*" she said. "You didn't like Ondine's? I haven't heard of anyone who didn't like it. Aunt Dinah and Uncle John loved it."

"Well, I didn't," said Leah. "It stunk."

"How can you say that?" said Robin.

Erin pulled on Robin's sweatshirt. "You can sit down now, Robin," she said. "Everyone's staring at you."

Robin shook her head. "But I can't *believe* she didn't like Ondine's!"

Leah made a face. "I told you I should stick to art. Why did you bother to ask me if you didn't want my opinion?"

"But Leah," said Erin, "what if Mr. Choux gets mad? Then what?"

"I don't know," said Leah. "Then he gets mad, I guess. Why are you blaming me? I'm the one who's got a stomachache!"

Robin turned to Amy and said, "Do we

39

have to run the review? Maybe we can just pretend we forgot to put it in."

Amy sighed. "When I saw Mr. Choux this afternoon he told me he couldn't wait to see what Leah wrote."

"He can wait, he can wait," said Robin.

"Anyway," said Erin, "we promised him we'd do the review if he ran an ad. It's not like we can get out of it that easily."

"So why doesn't one of us go to Ondine's and write another review?" said Robin. "Personally, I'd love to eat there."

Leah got upset. "You sent me because you trusted my taste. Just because you disagree now you can't throw out my review."

Amy wrung her hands. "She's right," she said. "I asked Leah to give her honest opinion and she did. Mr. Choux isn't going to be happy, but I think we should run it."

"Do we have to?" said Robin.

"Yes," said Amy. "Our first obligation is to the public. If we think they should know that the food at Ondine's is no good, then that comes first, not worrying about hurting Mr. Choux's feelings."

"Maybe this will make him want to improve it," said Leah.

"Maybe," said Erin.

"You don't seem too convinced," said Amy.

40

"I'm not," said Erin. "But I agree that we don't have any choice."

"So what do *you* think we should do?" asked Amy.

"I think we should go ahead and print it," she said. "Something tells me, though, we're making a big mistake."

Chapter Four

Amy spent the rest of that day and the next getting the paper ready to be printed. Some months were bigger for news than others, and this month was especially quiet. Their lead story was about Mrs. Richards, the town librarian, who was retiring after forty-two years. Amy couldn't imagine spending that long in one library, but if you saw Mrs. Richards, you could understand how she did it. Mrs. Richards looked like a librarian out of a movie—small, quiet, with gray hair and glasses. Amy liked her because she always recommended good books, but most kids, especially the boys, didn't like her at all.

On the second page were the restaurant review, Robin's gossip column, and the other monthly features, neatly arranged around

Leah's artwork. In honor of spring, Leah had covered the paper with drawings of leaping frogs wearing dark shades and high-top sneakers. Amy worried a little that it would make the paper not seem serious enough, especially after what they had written about Ondine's.

On late Thursday afternoon, everyone assembled in the treehouse to see the final layout. Robin was the first to arrive. "Wow," she said, holding up the layout. "Cool."

"Like it?" asked Amy.

"The frogs are really neat," said Robin. She turned to the second page. "Hey, you left something out of my gossip column. You left out that Mr. Eric and Ms. Underwood got caught kissing."

"I know," said Amy.

Robin's eyes narrowed. "How come?"

"I didn't think it was fair," said Amy. "Anyway, you never found out *why* they were kissing."

Robin made a long face. "It's not supposed to be news. It's gossip."

"It still needs to be substantiated," said Amy stubbornly.

Erin stuck her head inside the treehouse.

"What do *you* think?" asked Robin. "Should we leave out that Mr. Eric and Ms. Underwood were kissing?"

Erin looked at Amy and then back at Robin.

"Never mind," said Robin. "You always side with Amy." She headed for the ladder.

"Where are you going?" asked Amy.

"Where do you think?" said Robin. "I'm going to call up Mr. Eric and ask him."

"You are?" said Erin.

"Yep," said Robin. "See you in a few minutes."

While Robin was gone, Amy showed Erin the layout. "It looks nice," Erin said.

"What about the frogs? Too silly?"

"I like them," said Erin. They both stared at Leah's review. "I hope Mr. Choux doesn't take this the wrong way."

"Me too," said Amy.

Erin said, "Do you think the food was really that bad or do you think it was Leah's weird taste?"

"She *does* know a lot about food," said Amy.

Robin stuck her head back inside the treehouse. "I called him!"

"What did he say?" asked Amy.

Robin grinned. "Her kissed her all right!"

"And?" said Amy.

"It was Ms. Underwood's birthday. It was a birthday kiss."

"They aren't in love?" said Erin, disappointed.

45

"Nope," said Robin, acting as if she'd never heard that one. "Just friends. *Now* can we put it back in? I have more gossip, too. It was Ms. Underwood's thirtieth birthday. That's why she got the kiss."

"She doesn't look that old," said Erin. "She looks like a teenager."

"It's the way she dresses," said Robin knowingly. She took the layout out of Amy's hands and wrote the new information, including Ms. Underwood's age, into the gossip column. "There!" she said, handing it to Amy. "Now everything is perfect."

The girls distributed the paper that weekend, just like they always did. Then on Monday afternoon, right after Amy got home from school and before she even had a chance to look through the mail, the phone rang.

"Mademoiselle Evans?" said the unmistakable voice on the other end.

"Yes?" said Amy. Here goes, she thought.

"Mademoiselle Evans, I am horrified," he began.

Amy didn't say anything. How could she?

"For twenty years now, I have been a chef," Mr. Choux went on. "Never have I been so insulted. How could my pâté be too dry? What's too dry? Eh?"

Amy wasn't sure how to answer, especially since she'd never eaten pâté.

"What is the meaning of such a bad review?" Chief Choux demanded. "I was trying to help you girls. This isn't the way to treat peoples."

Amy tried her best to defend Leah. "Mr. Choux, our reporter eats out all the time. We asked her for her honest opinion and she gave it." Amy grimaced a little when she said it.

"Fine," said Mr. Choux. "Then I will give you *my* honest opinion. I'm canceling my ad."

"You're *what?*" Amy was stunned. She expected Mr. Choux to be angry, but she never thought he'd cancel his ad.

"You don't like my food, I don't like to advertise," he said bluntly. "Please send back all my monies."

"Your money? You can't do that! Just because you don't like what we wrote, you can't cancel. It doesn't work that way."

In an irritated voice he said, "Please, please. Don't insult me anymore. Just send back my monies."

"But—"

Mr. Choux slammed down the phone.

Amy took a deep breath. "Oh, boy." She dialed Erin's number. "We're in trouble," she said.

"What happened?"

Amy told her.

Erin gasped. "He canceled? He wants his money back? But we don't have it! We spent it on the typewriter. Listen, Amy. Tell him we'll do another review. A nice one."

Amy held the phone out. "What? Are you crazy?"

"What's wrong with that?"

"Mr. Choux doesn't own us, that's what's wrong with that. He asked us for a review and we gave it to him, like it or not."

"But we need his ad."

"Not that much we don't," said Amy angrily. "A newspaper is supposed to be independent."

Erin groaned. "Great, just great. Now what do we do? I told you Leah had weird taste. We should never have let her do the review. *She* should be the one who pays Mr. Choux back." She paused. "Wanna ask her?"

"Right. Thanks. That's real fair."

"She wrote the story."

Amy didn't say anything.

"Amy? You still there?"

Amy sighed. "I'll call her to tell her what happened," she said. "But I'm not asking her to pay. We'll just have to think of something else."

* * *

Naturally Leah was upset when Amy told her what happened. "I'm really sorry," Leah kept saying over and over. She sounded as if she were about to cry.

"You okay?" said Amy finally.

Now Leah really *did* start to cry. "I told you I didn't want to do this," she said. "Now everybody's m-m-mad at me and I was just doing my job. Nobody even told me they liked the writing."

Amy felt awful. "Oh, Leah. I'm sorry. The writing was really nice. It's not *your* fault you didn't like the food. How were we supposed to know he'd cancel his ad?"

Leah sniffled. "Where are we going to find the money?"

"Don't worry about it," said Amy. "You did the right thing."

"Thanks," said Leah. "That makes me feel better."

"I heard what happened," said Robin the next morning at the bus stop. She kicked a half-open trash bag back over to the curb. "This garbage is starting to get disgusting. Every morning it's the same thing."

"Did you talk to Mr. Sondra or Mr. Kresge yet?" asked Amy.

"I'll do it this weekend," she said. "The Sondras have been out of town. They went

49

to Washington, D.C., to see the cherry blossoms."

A passing car honked its horn.

"Look! It's Leah!" said Erin.

"Hi, guys," said Leah, hanging out the window. "Good news."

"What?" yelled Robin.

Leah shouted something about the treehouse.

Erin cupped her hands around her mouth. "What? We can't hear you."

Leah's car disappeared around the corner.

"Wonder what she was talking about?" said Robin.

"I think she wanted us to meet in the treehouse after school," said Amy. "It must be important."

"This better be good," said Robin later that afternoon. "Hilary went to the mall and I could've gone with her." Hilary was one of Robin's two big sisters.

Erin leaned out the treehouse window. "Where *is* she?" She polished off the last of the taco chips. "Maybe she didn't mean for us to meet here."

"Amy? Robin? Erin?" called someone from below.

"It's her," said Amy.

"Andre's with me," Leah said. "Can he come up?"

"Uh, sure," said Amy. She gave Erin and Robin a quizzical look. "I wonder why she wants to bring her father up?"

"Maybe she's scared we'll hit her or something," Robin whispered.

"Don't be stupid," hissed Erin.

Leah's black beret appeared first. "Hi," she said. She sounded cheerful. A good sign. "You okay, Andre?" she called down.

"Fine," boomed Leah's father.

Amy wasn't sure a grown-up could fit through the hatch, but Mr. Fox was pretty skinny so he made it without too much trouble.

"Hello, girls," he said, standing up. "Ow." He knocked his head on the ceiling. "Maybe I'd better sit down." Mr. Fox was wearing designer jeans and a purple sweater. He and Mrs. Fox always looked like they belonged in *Glamour* magazine, which was probably why Leah had taken to wearing all black lately. It was an act of rebellion.

Mr. Fox looked around the room. "This is quite amazing."

"Thank you," said Amy. She was dying to know what Mr. Fox was up to.

"I've got a small problem," he said, reading Amy's mind. "Maybe you can help me out. We're shooting a commercial next week for the Children's Castle." Mr. Fox's biggest client at his advertising agency was the Children's Castle, a giant toy store chain. "We need a location, though."

"You mean somewhere to shoot it?" said Robin.

"That's right," said Mr. Fox, looking around the treehouse some more. "I'm prepared to pay, of course."

Erin and Amy both gasped at once. "You mean . . . you mean you want to shoot your commercial *here*?" said Erin.

Mr. Fox grinned. "Not only that, I'd like you girls to be in it. Think you'd be interested?"

"Are you kidding?" shrieked Robin. "A chance to star in a TV commercial?"

"A way to pay back Mr. Choux?" said Erin.

"We'll do it!" said Amy. All three of them started hopping up and down and screaming at once.

"Glad this is going to work out," shouted Mr. Fox over the noise.

Amy gave Leah a big hug.

"It was Andre's idea," Leah said to her.

Erin and Robin were dancing around the room. "Wait until they hear about this at school," Robin said. "I can't wait to see Lark Hogan's face."

"Me neither," said Erin. "She's going to be so jealous."

"I wonder if people will start to recognize us," said Robin. "Maybe they'll ask us for our autographs wherever we go." She turned to Mr. Fox. "How much are you going to pay us? Is it enough to pay for college?"

Mr. Fox burst out laughing. "I hadn't planned on being that generous," he said. "How about twenty-five dollars apiece and one hundred dollars for the treehouse?"

"We'll take it," said Amy quickly.

Mr. Fox shook her hand. "Then it's a deal. We shoot next Thursday. I'll pay you at the end of the day. My assistant, Paula, will call with the details."

After everyone left, Amy went inside and tried phoning Mr. Choux. "Who's calling, please?" said the woman on the other end.

"Amy Evans from the *Treehouse Times*," she answered. There was a click and Amy was put on hold for a long time. Finally, the woman came back on. "He's busy," she said curtly. "May I take a message?"

Amy sighed. "Just tell him," she said, "that we'll have his money back next Thursday."

* * *

By that evening, everyone in Kirkridge had heard the news. The next morning, Amy and the others were waiting at the bus stop when Chelsea Dale, a fifth grader, came running up waving the real paper, the *St. Louis Post-Dispatch.* "You guuuys. Did you see?"

"It's already made the paper?" said Robin.

Chelsea stopped. "What are you talking about?" She leafed through until she found what she wanted. "Look!"

Amy, Erin, and Robin bent over. "What is it?"

"It's a review of Ondine's," said Chelsea. Her upper lip was perspiring like crazy.

"Let me see that," said Amy, pulling the paper away. "It's by Roberta Rall, the food critic," she said. She read the first sentence aloud. " 'If you like your pâté overdone and your fish underdone, perhaps you should try Ondine's in Kirkridge.' "

Erin snatched the paper from Amy's hand. "What does it really say?"

"That's what it really says," Amy answered. "See for yourself."

Erin's eyes skimmed the article. "Oh my gosh," she said.

"Do you think she talked to Leah?" said Robin.

It was such a stupid question, no one even bothered to answer her.

"Maybe Leah's taste wasn't so weird after all," said Amy.

"Or maybe they both have weird taste," said Erin. They all cracked up, but secretly Amy was glad Leah was off the hook.

Mr. Fox's assistant, Paula, called Amy that afternoon. She had a million questions, like where were the electrical outlets in the Evans' kitchen, how high off the ground was the treehouse, and how would they feel about having to miss a day of school for the shoot? Naturally Amy said missing school was no problem at all.

Paula also told Amy what they'd all be doing. She said that Amy and Erin would be demonstrating a rope ladder which they were going to hang from the hatch just for the commercial. Leah and Robin would be waving from the window, wearing satin baseball jackets which said Children's Castle on them. It all sounded good to Amy.

"Now," said Paula, "one last thing. We need some small children."

"You can ask Janice," said Amy. "She lives on Harrison. She does day-care." She gave Paula Janice's number. She heard someone pounding frantically on the kitchen door. "Excuse me, please."

It was Robin. "Can I talk to you?" she said. She looked pretty desperate.

"Just a minute," said Amy. She told Paula good-bye and hurried back. "What's wrong?"

"I can't do it. I can't be in the commercial," she said.

"Why not?" said Amy.

"Leah told me I'm supposed to model," she said.

"So?"

"So I've got to lose ten pounds before Thursday. I'll never make it."

"Relax," said Amy. "Paula said you'll be inside the window."

A wave of relief swept Robin's face. "I'll only be seen from the waist up?"

Amy nodded. "The jackets are pretty baggy, too."

"Whew," said Robin. "I'm glad you told me that. I read somewhere that being on TV makes you look ten pounds heavier. I mean, I don't want to seem paranoid or anything, but ten pounds is a lot on me."

"I understand," said Amy, suddenly wishing her hair were just a teeny bit longer. It took forever to grow.

Robin shoved her face further inside the kitchen. "What's that I smell? Cookies?"

"I'm making them as a surprise for Mom. Want one?"

"Sure!" said Robin. She headed for the

kitchen table and then stopped. "Are you absolutely positive I'll be in the window?"

"That's what Paula said."

Robin took three cookies and sat down. "Good," she said, biting into one. "Just checking."

Chapter Five

The next day was rainy, drizzly, and totally yucky. At the bus stop, everyone waited inside Chelsea's mother's van except for Roddy and Grant, who didn't care.

Mrs. Dale had put on the local radio station, and they all bounced up and down and sang along. It almost felt like camp.

"What are you wearing for the commercial?" Chelsea asked Amy between songs. Amy had been pretending to hum.

"I don't know," she answered. "I hadn't thought about it."

"You should," said Chelsea.

Amy glanced around at the others. "Why?"

"Because you can't just wear anything, that's why. Certain things look bad on TV."

Amy tugged her sweater. "Like what?"

Chelsea turned to Robin, who was sitting in the back seat. "What clothes did you say make you look bad?"

"White. No white. You'll be washed out. Solid colors are best."

"What else?" said Amy, trying to think what she had in her closet.

Robin studied Amy's face. "Ummm . . . maybe you can do something about your glasses."

"I can't see without them, remember?" said Amy.

Robin studied her some more. "Then how about your hair? Can you do something about your hair?"

"My bangs need trimming," said Amy. "That'll help."

"Maybe makeup will help, too. It'll bring out your eyes."

"Makeup?"

"What about *my* hair?" interrupted Erin. "Think it's okay?"

"Depends," said Robin. "You don't want to look like a boy."

Erin frowned. "I don't look like a boy!"

"Wait a second," said Robin. "I have an idea."

Amy wasn't sure she wanted to hear it, but to be polite she said, "What?"

"Maybe Hilary can help you guys."

60

"Help us what?" said Erin.

"You know. Help you figure out what to wear and how you should do your hair." Hilary worked at a hair salon on the weekends and she was also a prom princess, which must have been the reason Robin felt she was so qualified.

Amy hesitated. "I don't know . . ."

"Come on. It'll be worth it," said Robin. "She has great taste. She helps me pick out all my clothes."

Amy looked at Erin and Erin looked at Amy.

"Is that supposed to be a recommendation?" asked Erin.

"Very funny," said Robin. "Hilary had her colors done. She's very good at deciding what looks best on people."

"Oh, okay," said Amy reluctantly. "When can she come over?"

"Not today," said Robin. "She has cheerleading. Maybe tomorrow afternoon. She can go to your house first and then Erin's."

Erin held up her arms. "Hold it. Wait a second. I didn't say I wanted to do this."

"I'd think about it again if I were you," butt in Chelsea.

Erin gave her a dirty look.

Amy said, "Erin, if I'm doing it you have to, too."

"All right," she said, sighing. "But no

makeup. I hate makeup. It looks stupid on me and it makes my eyes itch.''

Amy looked out the window. "Bus!" she called. Everyone hopped out of the van and ran over to line up on the curb.

"Bye, Mom," called Chelsea. "Pick me up after school if it's still raining, okay?"

Mrs. Dale gave a little wave, honked her horn, and drove off.

It drizzled all day long. It was so wet, in fact, that no one was allowed to go outside during recess. Instead, they played dodgeball in the gym, which was always hot and noisy and not that much fun if you weren't great at dodgeball, which Amy wasn't. She was always worried her glasses were going to get broken.

When the bus left Amy and Erin off at their stop, it was still raining. "Want to come over?" Erin asked Amy. "Dad has a baby crow that someone just gave him. It's really cute.''

"Cool," said Amy. Erin's father was a biology teacher at Kirkridge High and people were always bringing him abandoned animals to take care of. As soon as he nursed them back, he'd always let them go.

They started up Erin's street. Because of the rain, hardly anyone was out.

"Do you think my hair looks like a boy's?" Erin said.

"No," said Amy. "Do you think my glasses look bad?"

"No," said Erin. They walked in silence for a few minutes. Erin suddenly stopped. "What's that?"

"What's what?"

"Shh," said Erin. "It sounds like someone calling."

They both listened. "Help, help me."

"It sounds like it's from over there," pointed Amy.

They ran toward the voice. "Help, I'm up here," the voice called.

"Up where?" shouted Erin, searching the trees.

"On the roof," the voice said again. "It's Sandy Appleby."

"Oh my gosh," gasped Amy. "He's hanging."

Erin and Amy stared. Sandy was Erin's neighbor, and he usually worked as a carpenter. Right now, though, he was dangling off his roof in some sort of harness.

They both rushed over. "Are you okay?" Amy called up.

"Fine," he yelled down. "I'm just glad someone came along. I've been hanging here for almost an hour. Do you think you could move that ladder back against the house? It slipped out from under me."

Erin and Amy quickly pushed the ladder back so that Sandy could climb onto it. "Thanks," he said, disconnecting the harness and climbing down. "Ahh, solid ground." He grinned at them both. "Good thing I put that harness on or I'd have been a goner."

"What were you doing up there?" asked Amy.

"Putting on a new roof," he said. Sandy was always doing things to his house when he was between jobs. He stared up at the gray sky and shook his head. "Any other day and there'd have been plenty of people around to hear me calling. I was beginning to think I was going to spend the rest of my life up there." He laughed out loud. "I sure am glad you two came along."

Erin blushed. She used to have a crush on Sandy, but that was before she started liking Matt O'Connor, who was more her age.

There was a pause in the conversation. "So how's the paper doing?" asked Sandy.

"Good," said Amy.

"Good," said Erin.

Sandy nodded. He had been their second Neighbor of the Month. "You going to write this up?"

"Can we?" said Amy.

"Absolutely," said Sandy. "I can see it now: Sandy Appleby Found Dangling Off Roof."

Erin blushed a second time and Amy giggled. Sandy *was* pretty cute. He had curly blond hair and muscled arms and he always wore T-shirts and jeans. His girlfriend's name was Amy, too, but Amy hadn't seen her for a while. Maybe they'd broken up.

Sandy started to wind up his rope.

"Quitting?" said Amy.

"I think I've had enough for one day," he said, laughing. He held out the rope. "Want to take my place?"

"No, thanks," said Amy. "Well, we'd better get going."

Sandy smiled. "Thanks for saving my life."

This time Amy blushed. "You're welcome," she said. She and Erin hurried away before they could get any more embarrassed.

When Amy's mother got home from work that evening, Amy was waiting for her in the kitchen. "Hi, Mom," she said.

Her mother looked up at the clock. "Hi, sweetie. Sorry I'm so late. Did you eat?"

"Patrick made cheese dogs in the microwave." Amy fidgeted around in her chair. "Can I ask you something?"

65

Her mother was digging through the pantry. "Sure. What?"

Amy waited until her mother had pulled out a box of cereal, poured herself a bowl, and sat down at the table.

"Do you think I could get contact lenses?"

Her mother looked at her. "Why do you want contacts?"

Amy ticked off the reasons. "They look better. They're easier because you don't have to keep taking them on and off all day. They improve your vision."

Her mother listened carefully. "Sounds like you've thought all this out."

"I have," said Amy hopefully. "Glasses can be a big pain."

"So can contacts," said her mother. "Having contact lenses is a big responsibility. They have to be cleaned, they have to be kept track of. It's not like a pair of glasses that you just take on and off."

"I know. I can be responsible."

Her mother looked at her. "What about if you're fooling around with your friends and you accidentally get knocked in the face?"

"That never happens," said Amy.

Her mother laughed. "It happened last week, remember? You told me that kid hit you with a basketball."

"He didn't hit my glasses," said Amy. "He hit my head."

66

"But what if it'd been your eyes? If you were wearing contacts, you would have been really hurt. I think you should wait a little longer."

Amy sighed. "All I ever do is wait."

Her mother finished her last bite of cereal. As she stood up, she gave Amy a kiss on the top of her head. "Don't worry, sweetie," she said. "Your time will come soon enough."

Amy made a face. She hated it when her mother said things like that.

"Now, where do you keep your sweaters?"

It was the next afternoon, and Amy and Erin were standing in Amy's bedroom with Hilary who had finally arrived a half hour late. "In the closet," Amy pointed.

Hilary cracked her gum and then threw open the closet door. The bracelets on her arm jangled together. "Show me where."

"Up there. On the shelf," said Amy.

Hilary nodded and reached inside the closet with her perfectly manicured pink nails. She had a new spikey blonde hairdo which Amy hadn't seen before. "Are these all you have?" she said, throwing Amy's four sweaters onto the bed.

"That's it," said Amy.

Hilary stood back. As she examined each one she kept up a running commentary. "Too bland," she said about the first one.

"Not enough color," she said about the second. She studied the third sweater for a long time. It was a sickening shade of purple and had been given to Amy last year for her birthday by her Aunt Linda. Hilary picked it up and held it against Amy's chest. "Nope. Wrong color." She cracked her gum again and threw the sweater into the reject pile.

"What about the last one?" asked Amy. The last one was actually her favorite. It was blue with little flowers across the top.

Hilary held the sweater up. "Not the greatest, but it'll do," she said.

"Oh, good," said Amy. "I was planning on wearing this one anyway."

"You're really more of an autumn type," Hilary went on. "Look. I'll show you." She steered Amy in front of the mirror. "See? Everyone is either a winter, spring, autumn, or summer. The colors of that season are what look best on you." She wrapped Amy's green bedspread around her shoulders and then draped Amy's brown jeans on top.

Erin giggled.

"See how these colors flatter your complexion?" she said.

Amy was having a hard time imagining, especially with her bedspread wrapped around her, but she nodded anyway.

"Now what can we do about your glasses?" said Hilary.

"I can't see without them," said Amy.

"Try," said Hilary. She pulled them off and started tugging on Amy's hair. "Your hair could use some highlighting," she said, weaving it into a French braid. "Or maybe a perm would help."

"It's still growing out," said Amy feebly.

"A perm is good if it's growing out," said Hilary. "We do perms at the salon all the time." Hilary fluffed up Amy's bangs with the hairbrush. "Much better. Now where do you keep your makeup?"

Amy pointed to some blue eye shadow and a raspberry-flavored lip gloss on the dresser. "I don't have that much."

"That's okay," said Hilary. "We'll borrow from your mom. Blue isn't in your color palette anyway." She headed out to the hall.

Erin and Amy looked at each other.

"Come on, guys," Hilary called. "I haven't got all day."

In the bathroom, Hilary already had the medicine cabinet open and was pulling things down. She stopped for a moment to read the prescription medicine labels and then piled all the makeup onto the sink counter. "Now don't panic," she said to Amy. "I'm only going to do a little eye shadow and some mascara, okay?"

Amy peeked at her French braid. It looked pretty good from what she could see, which wasn't much since she wasn't wearing her glasses.

"Close your eyes," said Hilary. She dabbed some copper eyeshadow on the corner of Amy's eyes. "See where I put that? Not all over, okay?"

Hilary pulled out the mascara. "Look up. Now look down. You're all done. Nice, huh?"

Amy turned to Erin. "Not bad," said Erin to Amy's great relief.

"Now who's next?" said Hilary. She cracked her gum.

"Me," said Erin.

Hilary eyed her up and down. "Winter," she said. "Stick with reds, blues, pale yellows." She riffled through Mrs. Evans' eye shadows. "Close, please."

To Amy's surprise, Erin dutifully closed.

"Open," said Hilary. "Look up. Look down. Finished."

Erin peered into the mirror. "What about my hair?"

"It needs some volume," said Hilary, grabbing a hairbrush. She sprayed it with some hair spray she found underneath the sink and then brushed it out and up. "Much better," she said when she was finished.

Erin stared at Amy. "Well?"

"It looks nice," said Amy, straining her eyes.

Hilary grinned and cracked her gum. "I

told you I wouldn't overdo it. Makeovers are my specialty."

As soon as Hilary left, Amy put her glasses back on so she could *really* see what she looked like.

"Let's go for a walk around the block," said Erin, patting down her hair a little. "Maybe someone will notice."

"Okay," said Amy. She and Erin hurried outside and started slowly up Washington Street. Unfortunately, the first people they ran into were Roddy and Grant.

"*Aaaaaa*, aliens," screamed Roddy.

Erin patted down her hair some more. "Very funny, Roddy."

"What happened to you guys?" he said. He leaned closer. "Fess up, Evans."

Amy's eyes narrowed. "Ha, ha. You're so funny I forgot to laugh."

Erin tugged on her arm. "Come on, Amy. Let's get out of here."

They turned and saw Sandy headed toward them with an armload of lumber. "Oh, great," groaned Amy. For one frantic minute she wished she'd never let Hilary do this to her.

Sandy staggered past. "Going to a party?" he asked.

"Not really," Amy muttered. Why had she ever let Hilary talk her into this?

71

"You look nice," he said.

Amy gasped. "I do?" she said. "I mean, we do?"

Erin fluffed out her hair.

"Yeah," Sandy shouted over his shoulder. "Very grown-up."

Amy and Erin looked at each other. "Very grown-up?" whispered Erin. "What's that supposed to mean?"

"It means," said Amy, arching her eyebrows, "that fall and winter look good on us, dahling." They both cracked up and giggled all the way back to Amy's house.

Chapter Six

The first thing Amy noticed Monday morning at the bus stop was that Erin had fluffed out her hair again.

"Your hair looks nice," she said to her as she walked up.

Erin glanced around and then said under her breath, "Do you think it's too much?"

"You can hardly tell," said Amy.

At that moment, Robin ran over. "Big news!" she said, waving her book bag. "Have I got some news!"

"What?" said Amy. "What is it?"

Robin stopped to catch her breath. "Mr. Sondra," she said between puffs, "is suing Mr. Kresge!"

"What do you mean?" asked Erin.

"He's taking him to court," said Robin. "What do you think I mean?"

"Why?" gasped Amy.

"Disturbing personal property," Robin said. "He said he's sick of Hefty getting into his garbage and digging in his vegetable garden. He said he's had to call the police three times already. But that's not all."

"What else?" asked Chelsea, who had managed to worm her way into the middle.

"Mr. Kresge denies the whole thing," she said. "He said that Hefty hates garbage. He wasn't even in town one of the nights that Mr. Sondra claimed he saw Hefty in the trash. And about the fight? He said Hefty doesn't fight. He's a big chicken."

"Weird," said Erin.

"It gets weirder," said Robin. "We saw Hefty fighting, right? And Hilary swears that she saw Hefty knocking over trash cans the other night when she was coming home from a date. But when I asked Mr. Kresge about it, he said he was asleep and Hefty was in the house." She dug around in her book bag for a minute and then pulled out a wrinkled sheet of paper. "Here. I wrote the whole thing down."

Amy took Robin's story and started to read it. Robin looked anxiously over Amy's shoulder and noisily sucked on a caramel chewie.

Amy rubbed her ear. "Do you mind?" she said.

Robin backed off. "Sorry." She waited until Amy had finished. "Well? Pretty good, don't you think?"

"It's great," said Amy. "You got both sides this time. I think there's more to the story that we don't know yet, though."

Robin beamed. "That's why I'm going to keep following it," she said. "Something's not right."

Chelsea interrupted. "Here comes the bus! Let's go, guys!"

Amy handed Robin back her story. "Keep it up, Robin."

"Thanks," she said. "I will."

That afternoon after school, Paula called Amy. "We've decided to schedule a rehearsal for tomorrow since we're working with so many children," she said. Amy wondered if that meant her. She always referred to herself as a kid, not a child. Child made her sound like a baby. "Can you get out of school a little early?" Paula asked. "Maybe two o'clock?"

"I think so," said Amy, sounding her most grown-up. "All I'm missing is gym. Want me to tell the others?"

"I think I've left messages or reached them all," Paula said. "Let's see. We have you,

Erin, Robin, Leah, and the three children from day-care."

"Oh, good," said Amy. "Which ones did you get?"

"Keri, Andrew, and Cole," said Paula. "I hope they behave."

"They will," said Amy. "They're really cute." She thought of something else. "Should we wear what we're going to wear for the real thing?"

"Please," said Paula. "Our stylist will be there."

Amy started to get excited all over again. Just think! Everyone in St. Louis, all two million people, would be watching them on TV. Maybe there was some way she could get a copy of the newspaper into the commercial. She reminded herself to make sure there were plenty of extra copies lying around.

"Don't worry about cleaning anything up," Paula was saying. "We want to keep the flavor of a kids' backyard treehouse as accurate as possible."

"Okay," said Amy. "I won't." She remembered something else. "Is it okay for my dad to mow the lawn? It's getting sort of long."

"That's fine," said Paula cheerfully. "You probably won't see much of it, but it's a good idea anyway."

After Amy hung up the phone, she did two

things. First, she wrote a note to her father, reminding him to cut the grass. Next, she wrote a note to her mother, asking her to call the principal's office for permission to leave school early. When she was finished, she went up to the bathroom to practice her makeup some more. She promised herself that after dinner she would go back outside and make sure the inside of the treehouse was picked up. Maybe she'd even do a little dusting, just to be sure it didn't look too gross up there.

It was the next afternoon. Outside Amy's house, Mr. Fox held up a bullhorn and said, "Quiet, everyone. I need your attention, please."

Amy looked up from the Pogo ball she'd been bouncing around on for most of the last hour. The French braid Leah had fixed in her hair was nearly out, and she was sure the makeup had all been rubbed off. It was okay, though, because the stylist, Kathy, had already checked her out and said she was fine for Thursday. "Ow!" Now Amy got hit in the back for the third time by a stupid dart thing that Robin refused to share. Amy grabbed her glasses just in time. "Do you mind?"

"Sorry," said Robin.

Strewn around the yard were about fifteen brand-new toys from the Children's Castle which Mr. Fox had brought with him when he'd first arrived. "Here, kids," he'd said, dumping them all in a huge pile. "Play with these until we get organized."

Amy had never seen so many great toys. There were games like Frisbee tag and dunk ball and there was a life-sized blow-up alligator that made noise and there was even a remote control airplane, which Erin had spent a long time trying to fly through the treehouse window. The whole thing was a riot.

"I think we're finally ready to begin, kids," said Mr. Fox. He handed the bullhorn to a short man named Marc, who was the director.

"Thanks for your patience," said Marc. "Now that Kathy's had a chance to see everyone and the rope ladder's been installed, let's start figuring out where everyone will go."

"I'm in the window," said Robin, throwing the dart game onto the grass and heading for her position. "Come on, Leah." Hilary had done a great job on Robin's makeup. Even Kathy said so.

Marc watched Robin and Leah take their places and then said, "Now, why don't we have the three little ones over by the ladder?" Keri, Andrew, and Cole stopped fighting over the alligator long enough to get situated. "Here, Cole," said Marc. "You hold the airplane and Andrew can hold the darts."

Cole nodded silently. Usually he never shut up. Maybe all the excitement had him a little overwhelmed.

Amy noticed that several of the neighbors, including Sandy Appleby, had come over to watch. Pretty soon school would be out and then *everyone* would be here. While she waited for Marc to tell her what to do, Amy jotted down some notes in her reporter's notebook: "played w/toys for a long time while Kathy checked our outfits . . . makeup looked good . . . lots of people came to watch . . . Sandy—" She saw Marc heading toward her and she quickly crossed out Sandy's name. She didn't want anyone to get the wrong idea.

"Why don't you climb onto that rope ladder now?" Marc was saying to her and Erin. Erin was already dangling.

Amy didn't know what made her do it, but she suddenly pulled off her glasses and tucked them into her back pocket. She managed to make it across to the ladder without falling flat on her face.

"Amy! Where are your glasses?" hissed Erin.

"I took them off," Amy said. She carefully felt for the first rung and hauled herself up.

"Can you see?" whispered Erin.

"Of course not," Amy said.

They both began to giggle.

"Quiet, please," said Mr. Fox. He put a cassette into a portable tape recorder and the Children's Castle theme song came on. "We have what you're looking for. Toys galore and so much more."

Amy could swear she saw her big brother Patrick watching from inside the house. Or maybe it was her mother's Easter lily.

Marc had picked up the bullhorn. "Now pay attention please," he said. "As the jingle starts, please just sing along, will you? I want to hear you loud and clear."

Amy panicked. "Sing? No one said anything about singing."

"Just pretend," whispered Erin.

"What if he can tell?" said Amy.

Erin giggled. "Would you rather have him listen to your singing?"

"Let's try it," said Marc. "Ready?"

Amy nodded and lip-synched along. Erin was right. Nobody noticed.

They practiced the whole thing—the song, the little wave Marc asked them to do at the end, and the big smile—about ten more times. It seemed to Amy that everyone had the routine down after about the third time, but Marc still had them do it a bunch more. Finally he said, "Okay, looks good. Let's stop. We don't want it to be stale."

Amy strained her eyes to see if anyone was still watching them.

"See you all Thursday morning," Marc said. "I expect you on the set at eight sharp."

"Eight in the morning?" said Robin from upstairs.

"Is that a problem?" asked Marc.

"It's so early," said Robin.

Marc laughed. "Welcome to TV, kids."

That night Amy was awakened again by the sound of garbage cans being knocked over. She sat up in bed and felt for her glasses. Crash! Another one. She ran to the window. Next door at the Caspers' she could vaguely make out what looked like a large dog bent over a trash bag. The wind was howling, causing the trees to bend and sway.

Amy threw on a sweatshirt and a pair of jeans over her nightshirt and quietly tiptoed out into the hall. As she snuck past Patrick's room she heard him say, "Where do you think you're going?"

"Investigating," she said. "I'll be back in a minute."

Patrick pulled his pillow over his head and rolled back over.

Amy let herself out the kitchen door, making sure she left it unlocked. The howling

81

had stopped now, making the air seem crisp and still. Thunder rumbled in the distance.

Amy quietly crept next door. Beside the curb she saw the unmistakable tail of a large black dog wagging. "Hefty!" she hissed. "Get over here!"

Hefty kept chewing away on what looked like a large chicken bone.

"Hefty! Come!"

When Hefty ignored her a second time, Amy walked over and grabbed him by the collar. "What's gotten into you?"

Hefty looked up and growled menacingly.

"Oh no!" gasped Amy. "You're not Hefty!" She quickly let go of the dog's collar. If he wasn't Hefty, then who was he? She waited until the dog had finished the chicken bone and then carefully read the tag on his collar. "SHANE. I belong to D. Harmon, 429 Tyler St." Tyler was a few blocks from here, and Amy didn't recognize the owner's name.

Shane wagged his tail and trotted off toward the Davises' house. "Hey, wait!" said Amy. "Where do you think you're going?" Amy watched as Shane sniffed the Davises' two garbage cans and then expertly knocked them both over. "So it's *you!*" she said, watching him tear into the trash. "Poor Hefty's been taking the blame and it's been you all along."

Shane nudged an asparagus spear out of the way and ripped through another plastic bag. "Bad dog," said Amy. She felt a large raindrop hit her nose. Shane looked at her and growled. Another raindrop and then another plunked onto the sidewalk. The wind had started up again.

"I'm calling your owner tomorrow," she said, hurrying home. A large bolt of lightning flashed across the sky. Amy made it back through the kitchen door just as it began to pour.

Back in bed, Amy listened to the thunder and lightning grow louder and the rain pound against the roof. Usually she loved thunderstorms, but she had a funny feeling about this one. She heard her mother get up and close the windows. Patrick must have been up, too, because she heard her mother say something to him about the state of his room.

Suddenly a huge crack of lightning shook the whole house. Amy's alarm clock went dead. Amy jumped out of bed. "Mom, where are you?" she called.

"Out here, honey."

Amy rushed into the dark hall. "Did the electricity go out?"

Her mother nodded. "Frightened?" She put her arms around Amy.

Amy's father and Patrick both showed up

83

with flashlights. "Pretty cool, huh?" said Patrick. "Did you feel the whole house shake?" He shined the flashlight on his chin and laughed like a monster. "Ah, ha, ha."

Amy's father turned on his transistor radio. "We have a tornado watch in the area," the announcer was saying. Amy was glad her parents didn't know she'd just been outside. She'd wait until tomorrow to tell them about Hefty.

"Honey," said Amy's mother to her father, "are all the car windows up? Did we leave anything out in the yard?"

Another bolt of lightning ripped through the sky. This time it was followed by a huge cracking sound. "Uh oh," said Amy's father. He ran to the window in his bedroom.

"What was that?" said Amy's mother.

"Sounds like something got hit." He dashed down the stairs.

"Wait for us, Dad," yelled Patrick.

They all followed him to the kitchen, where he carefully opened the back door.

"Do you see anything?" asked Amy's mother anxiously. They all clustered around. The air had a funny burnt smell to it, like someone had been outside barbecuing or something.

Amy's father flashed the beam of light around the yard. "Aha!" he said. He gave a grim nod. "Sure do."

Amy edged around her father. "What? What is it?" She suddenly gasped. "Oh, no!" she cried. "Look! It's the treehouse! It's been hit!"

Chapter Seven

Amy grabbed the flashlight from her father and shined it on the treehouse.

Patrick gave a low whistle. "Wow."

A big gash ran right through the middle of it where a giant branch had fallen from above. "I'm going over there," said Amy. She felt her father grab her arm.

"No, you're not."

"But all our stuff is in there," Amy said with a wail. "It'll get ruined in the rain."

Amy's mother put her hands on her shoulders. "It can wait until tomorrow," she said gently. "Until the storm passes."

"What about the typewriter?" said Amy. "It'll rust up." She gave a cry. "Oh, no! I just remembered something else. What about the commercial? Does this mean we can't do it?"

Patrick said, "Doesn't look too good."

Amy felt the tears start down her cheeks. "But we were all ready," she said. "We practiced and everything."

Her mother gave her a quiet hug. "There'll be other opportunities," she said.

"But *now* is when we need the money," sobbed Amy. "I promised Mr. Choux. It's not fair."

"There, there," said her mother soothingly. "It's not the end of the world. Mr. Choux can wait. And the treehouse can be repaired. Right, David?"

"We'll do it this weekend," said her father, trying to look cheerful.

Amy stared out the door. "This weekend!" she said. "This weekend is too late. Right now is when we need it."

The next morning Amy awoke to the sound of a chain saw. "The treehouse!" she said, hurrying to the window. Thankfully, no one was cutting it down, but seeing the damage the lightning had caused put her in shock all over again. Pieces of splintered wood and debris were spread across the lawn, and a huge gaping hole in the treehouse wall stared her in the face. The branch that had snapped from above was so long that one end of it rested on the ground.

Amy thought she saw someone moving

around behind the bottom of the branch. She threw on some old clothes and hurried outside to get a closer look.

"Hi there." Sandy Appleby stepped out from behind the fallen branch carrying a big chain saw.

Amy gulped. "Oh. Hi. It's you!" Why hadn't she thought to brush her hair? Or her teeth? She always brushed her teeth first thing. At least she wasn't wearing her pajamas.

Sandy started up the saw and began cutting off another piece. "Thought you could use some help here," he shouted over the noise.

"Wow. Thanks," Amy shouted back. "That's really nice of you." She was careful not to open her mouth too wide.

Sandy stopped the saw. "Weren't you supposed to make a TV commercial here today?"

Amy felt the knot in her stomach come back. "Tomorrow," she said. She stared up at the fallen branch. The hole it had made in the treehouse let her see right in. Her chair was lying in two pieces on its side. "I'm going up," she said.

Sandy kicked a freshly cut-off section of the branch out of the way. "Probably a good idea. Need some help?"

"I'm okay," said Amy grimly. She scrambled up the ladder and prepared herself for the worst.

Surprisingly, things were not that bad. Aside from the chair, the branch had missed everything except Amy's pig calendar, which had been hanging on the wall over the card table and was now lying in a soggy crumpled heap on the floor.

"Careful up there," she heard Sandy call.

"Don't worry," said Amy. She slid over to where the hole stood and peeked down at him.

"How's it look?"

"Pretty good except for my chair and my pig calendar."

"You're lucky."

"I know." To be sure she was right, she ducked down and crawled around the branch and over to the card table. The type-writer was dry. Even better, it was still in one piece. Still, where were they going to get the money for a new chair? And what about repairs to the treehouse? That was going to cost, too.

"Oh, my *gosh!* This is terrible!" someone yelled from below.

Amy crawled back over to the hole. "Robin! How'd *you* get here?"

"I don't believe this," Robin said, staring up at her. "I thought I heard lightning hit something last night and then when I fell back asleep I actually *dreamed* it was the treehouse. When I woke up this morning I couldn't stop thinking about it so I came over to see if it was true." She took a deep breath. "This is awful. What are we going to do? What about the commercial?"

"I guess we can't do it," said Amy. "We can't do anything."

Robin groaned. "Figures! Now we'll never be famous. Do Erin and Leah know yet?"

"Nobody does."

Robin shook her head. "I still can't believe I dreamed this. Maybe I'm psychic or something." She suddenly noticed Sandy standing there with his chain saw. "Are you cutting the branch up?"

"Trying to."

Robin looked up at the hole. "What about the treehouse? Can you fix it?"

"Robin!" said Amy.

Sandy shook his head. "Not by tomorrow, if that's what you mean. It's too much work for one person. That whole side has to be torn down."

"Well, what if we helped you?" asked Robin. "Do you think if we all helped we could get the treehouse fixed in time?"

Amy climbed down the ladder and hurried over. She couldn't believe Robin.

Now Robin was saying, "I'm really good with a hammer. So's Erin."

"Aren't you forgetting something?" said Sandy with a grin. "You have school today, remember?"

"So?" said Robin. "We can do it when we get home. How long can it take? The hole isn't *that* big."

Sandy shrugged. "You'd be surprised," he said. "You're talking about a new roof, a new side . . . Maybe if I can get the branch removed while you're at school, *maybe* when you get back we'll be able to put it all together in time for tomorrow. No guarantees, though."

Amy looked at Sandy. "Are you sure you want to do this?" she asked. "I mean, don't you have somewhere else to work today?"

"Hey," he said, "This *is* work. Besides, I owe you one, right?"

Amy's face turned pink. For once, she was glad she had her glasses to hide behind. "I'll call Leah and Erin."

"And I'll see who else we can get," said Robin. "Don't worry, guys. We'll get it done. I know we will."

By the time Amy got home from school, word about the treehouse had spread through the neighborhood and a small crowd of helpers had already gathered. Over by the garage, Mr. Sondra and Erin's older brother, Christopher, were busy stacking the logs Sandy had cut up. Janice had Keri, Andrew, and Cole picking up sticks on the lawn. Up in the treehouse, Amy could see her brother Patrick helping Sandy pry off the smashed side.

Amy ran over to the treehouse. "Patrick! What are *you* doing here?" Normally all Patrick cared about anymore was his motorcycle.

"What does it look like?" he said. "Dad and I built this treehouse, remember?"

"Yes, but . . ."

All of a sudden, Mr. Kresge appeared through the shrubs. "Hi, Amy," he boomed. Mr. Kresge was big and tall like the Jolly Green Giant. "Heard you needed some help over here."

"You did?" said Erin, staring up at him.

Mr. Kresge nodded solemnly. "Sandy gave me a call. Just show me what you need. I can't climb anymore but I can still drive a nail."

Amy grinned and pointed up. Before Mr. Kresge retired he had been a carpenter. "Sandy's in charge."

Mr. Kresge noticed Mr. Sondra over by the garage. "What's *he* doing here?"

Amy suddenly remembered about last night. "Uh, helping," she said. She searched the yard for Robin. Wait till she told her what she'd found out!

Mr. Kresge shook his bushy gray head

back and forth. "Just keep him out of my way," he growled.

Sandy swung down. "Hey, Bob, thanks for coming."

Mr. Kresge stared right at Mr. Sondra. "Ordinarily, Sandy, I wouldn't have."

"Bob," said Sandy in a teasing voice, "we're here to help fix the treehouse, remember?"

"Hmpf," said Mr. Kresge. He sounded as grouchy as Mr. Sondra.

At that moment, Leah showed up. She was wearing a pair of painter's overalls which looked like she'd painted herself. "Hi, guys," she said breathlessly. "I got here as fast as I could. We had a rehearsal this afternoon for our Spring Fling." She took one look at the treehouse. "Wow."

"You should have seen it this morning," said Robin, strolling up with a bag of pretzels.

"Robin! Where were you?" asked Amy.

"Your kitchen," said Robin, waving the pretzel bag. "I was feeling a little faint so I decided to find something to eat."

"I need to talk to you," said Amy, pulling her aside. "I discovered something last night," she whispered. "It's about your story about Hefty."

"What about it?" said Robin.

Sandy interrupted. "How 'bout some help

up here?" he called. He and Patrick were trying to pull a large sheet of plywood into the treehouse.

"I'll tell you the rest in a minute," said Amy. She ran over and grabbed the other end of the plywood with Mr. Kresge.

"Okay, fellas," he said. "Lift."

The sheet of plywood wobbled up and then suddenly tilted backwards. "Ooops! Look out!" shouted Mr. Kresge. The plywood fell to the ground with a crash, bouncing to one side and barely missing Amy.

"Eeek," she screamed.

"Oh, golly. I'm sorry," said Mr. Kresge.

Sandy leapt out of the tree like Robin Hood. "Are you all right?"

"Uh huh," said Amy, wishing she'd at least have gotten a bruise. "Are you?"

Sandy nodded and rubbed his leg. "We shouldn't have tried to lift that board without more help."

Amy stared at the plywood. Just their luck! A large crack ran from one side to the other.

"Hey, don't worry," said Sandy, reading her thoughts. "I've got more of this in my garage." He headed off toward his house. "Bob, maybe you can start measuring that roof piece."

"Will do," said Mr. Kresge, giving a little wave.

Amy suddenly noticed Mr. Sondra standing right next to her.

"Hi, Mr. Sondra," she said. "It was nice of you to come help.

Mr. Sondra wasn't listening. "You know," he said to her, "there's a better way to do that."

Sandy turned around. "Do what, Herman?"

"Lift that wood up. What you need is a pulley."

Mr. Kresge frowned. "No, we don't," he said. "We just need another person."

Mr. Sondra shrugged. "Suit yourself."

Mr. Kresge's eyes narrowed. "Don't start with me, Herman." Everyone became very quiet. Amy wondered whether Mr. Kresge and Mr. Sondra were going to start another fight.

Instead, Robin surprised everybody by butting in and saying, "He's only trying to help, Mr. Kresge."

"Ha!" said Mr. Kresge. "For fifty years now, Herman Sondra has been trying to help. He told me how to build my house, he told me how to raise my kids, he told me why I should buy a Chrysler and not a Ford. Heck, he'd tell me how to blow my nose if I'd let him."

"Baloney!" said Mr. Sondra.

"It's true," said Mr. Kresge. "Isn't that

what this darn lawsuit is all about? You dreaming up ways to get back at me?"

"I'm not dreaming," said Mr. Sondra. "I saw Hefty with my own eyes."

Amy decided it was time to say something. "Wait a minute," she interrupted. "Hefty's not the one getting into the garbage. It's Shane, a dog who lives on Tyler. I watched him doing it last night. He looks just like Hefty."

Mr. Kresge's eyes gleamed. "Aha! You see? You see? What was I saying all along? It has nothing to do with Hefty. Hefty doesn't like garbage. And he doesn't dig holes in yards, either. You're still trying to get back at me, Herman, over those gosh darned tomatoes!"

"I am not," said Mr. Sondra. He folded his arms.

Robin whispered into Amy's ear, "What tomatoes?"

"Ten years," crowed Mr. Kresge, "and you still can't believe my tomatoes beat yours out, can you?"

"What are you guys talking about?" said Sandy.

Mr. Kresge's eyes scanned the whole group, which by now had clustered around. "Ten years ago, Herman bet me I couldn't grow tomatoes as big as his but I showed him. Mine were twice the size, right, Herman?"

"Not twice," said Mr. Sondra.

"He's been looking for a way to get back at me ever since," said Mr. Kresge.

"You cheated!" yelled Mr. Sondra.

"Did not!" said Mr. Kresge. "I won fair and square. Just because I never grew anything before didn't mean I couldn't win."

Mr. Sondra's face was turning purple. "You stole my secret fertilizer, didn't you?" he sputtered. "Admit it, Bob. You never would have won if you hadn't snuck into my garage for my fertilizer."

Mr. Kresge suddenly stopped. "I what?" he thundered.

Mr. Sondra pointed a long, bony finger at him. "You stole my fertilizer."

Mr. Kresge threw back his head and started to laugh. He laughed and laughed and laughed and laughed, which was very weird since no one else knew why he was laughing. Finally, he said, "You mean to tell me, you've been mad at me all these years because you thought I stole your secret fertilizer?" He started laughing again.

"Well, didn't you?" said Mr. Sondra, not as confidently this time.

"Heck, no, Herman," said Mr. Kresge. "Joe Schmidt gave me that tomato fertilizer."

Mr. Sondra's mouth suddenly twisted into a surprised expression. "Joe Schmidt!" he said. "Joe Schmidt?" Now it was his turn to burst out laughing. "Don't tell me you fell for that fertilizer story!" he said. He was grinning ear to ear. "How much did you pay for that stuff? An arm and a leg, I bet."

Mr. Kresge shifted from one foot to the other. "Why? What was wrong with it?"

Erin whispered into Amy's ear, "Who's Joe Schmidt?"

"He died two years ago," Amy whispered back. "He lived on Lincoln."

"Rabbit manure!" said Mr. Sondra. "That's all it was! He shoveled it out from under that rabbit cage he kept in his yard."

Mr. Kresge's eyes narrowed. "Well it worked, didn't it? So what if it cost me?"

But Mr. Sondra wasn't listening. "He tried to sell me that phony secret fertilizer one time. Told me he paid five hundred dollars for the recipe. I was too smart for him, though. I knew exactly what it was."

"It worked, didn't it?" Mr. Kresge repeated.

"Rabbit pellets," Mr. Sondra snorted. He turned to Sandy. "Say, did you want me to put that hatch on? It should be done before you put the roof back."

"Uh, sure," said Sandy.

He handed Mr. Sondra the figures, and Mr. Sondra got started. "Now let's see . . ."

Robin turned to the other girls and

scratched her head. "I don't get it," she said in a low voice. "What do tomatoes have to do with Hefty?"

"Nothing," said Amy, still trying to sort the story out herself. "Let me see if I got this right. All this time Mr. Sondra was looking for a way to get back at Mr. Kresge for winning the tomato-growing contest."

Erin nodded. "That's right," she said. "And when he thought he saw Hefty in his garbage it was his big chance."

"Oh, I get it!" said Robin. "Only it wasn't Hefty. It was that other dog."

"Shane," said Leah.

"But Mr. Sondra didn't care," said Amy. "He was mostly mad because he thought Mr. Kresge stole his secret fertilizer recipe."

"Only he hadn't," said Erin.

Robin shook her head back and forth. "It just goes to show you," she said, "that you never really know."

"That's for sure," said Erin. She glanced over at Mr. Sondra and Mr. Kresge. "Now maybe they can be friends again."

"I hope so," said Amy. "I like it when people make up."

Chapter Eight

Just as Amy predicted, after Mr. Sondra and Mr. Kresge had their big fight, the work got done a lot faster. Mr. Kresge even made a joke at one point that Mr. Sondra laughed at. It was about how many idiots it takes to screw in a light bulb which Amy had heard a million times, but Mr. Sondra acted as if he hadn't.

Around six o'clock, Amy's parents got home from work. Having them there really helped, especially since Amy's father had built the treehouse in the first place. By then, Janice and the little kids had all gone home, but Christopher and Patrick were still around, and even Chelsea Dale, who normally did nothing but pester people, showed up to help out. Mrs. Evans ordered pizza for everyone.

At seven-thirty, just as it was getting dark, Sandy and Amy's father finished putting in the last nail. "That's it!" said Sandy, waving to them from the roof of the treehouse.

"Hooray!" Robin shouted.

Leah tossed her beret in the air. "I'll go call Andre."

"Come on inside, everyone, for ice cream," said Mrs. Evans. "Please excuse the condition of the house." Her mother always said that, even when the house was clean.

Amy walked over to where Sandy was putting away his tools. She smoothed out her sweatshirt and took off her glasses. "Thanks for helping," she said. "We never would have finished without you."

"My pleasure," said Sandy.

Amy smiled. She liked how he said, "My pleasure." It sounded like something a knight would have said to a lady-in-waiting. "Do you want some ice cream? Mom bought two flavors—mint chocolate chip and butter pecan."

Sandy laughed. "I guess I could work up an appetite for some butter pecan."

"Okay. See you inside," said Amy. She waited until she was almost to the kitchen door before putting her glasses back on.

* * *

That night, Amy could hardly sleep. Tomorrow, after the commercial was shot, everybody in Kirkridge would know who they were. She wondered if she'd get asked for her autograph. It also occurred to her that the paper should probably do a story on how they shot the commercial. She got out of bed, put on her desk light, and wrote down on the Don't Forget pad she kept on her desk, "1. Do story about the commercial."

After she got back in bed, she remembered something else. She walked back over to her desk and wrote, "2. Call Shane's owner and tell him about the garbage. Maybe write story?" Under that she put, "3. Pay Mr. Choux!"

Thinking about Mr. Choux made Amy wince. Even though she knew she had done the right thing by printing the review and refusing to change it, the fact that he canceled his ad and wouldn't talk to them really bothered her. It didn't seem fair for an adult to treat them that way. She dreaded having to go into the restaurant to pay him back. Maybe she could mail him his refund instead.

Amy got back into bed again but she still wasn't sleepy so she tried on her outfit she was going to wear for the commercial, just to be sure she hadn't grown or anything. It looked pretty good, especially when she took off her glasses.

She neatly laid everything out and climbed back in bed. She was finally starting to feel a little tired. Good thing. Tomorrow was going to be a long day.

"Rise and shine!" said Mrs. Evans.

Amy slowly opened one eye. Without her glasses, she could barely make her mother out, but she appeared to be holding something. "What's going on?" she asked.

She put on her glasses and the room came into focus. Her mother was holding a tray with breakfast on it. "Is that for me?"

"Sure is," said her mother. "I wanted you to start the day off right."

Amy rubbed her eyes. "Wow. Pop Tarts and orange juice."

Her mother beamed. "I wish I could be here today to watch everything."

"You'll watch us on TV," said Amy.

"Not the same," said her mother. She leaned over and gave Amy a kiss. "Sorry I have to leave so early. Busy day. I'll be thinking of you."

Amy took a bite of her Pop Tart. "Thanks, Mom."

The backyard was already buzzing with activity when Amy stepped outside not long after. Heavy electric cables ran from the kitchen out to the tree. A couple of guys in jeans and T-shirts were carrying equipment back and forth from a van parked in the driveway. Amy walked up to her father and Patrick, who were talking to Andre.

"I must say, I'm thrilled that we were still able to use the treehouse," Andre was saying. "Sandy did a great job."

"He's a nice kid," said Mr. Evans.

"Hi, Mr. Fox," said Amy. "I'm ready."

"Good for you," said Leah's father. He had on his ascot. "Marc has a sign-in sheet over by the van. When you're done, find Kathy and have her check your hair and makeup."

Amy ran off in search of the sign-in sheet and the rest of the girls. She was glad her father and Patrick hadn't said anything embarrassing to her about her hair or makeup.

Amy found Erin, Leah, and Robin by the van, talking to some guy with long blond hair and an earring. Amy heard him telling the others that he was from L.A. and he couldn't wait to get back.

"I'm from L.A. too," said Erin. "Reseda."

"That's not L.A.," said the guy. "That's the valley."

Mr. Fox rushed over. "Girls," he interrupted, "let Kent do his job."

Kent said something under his breath and walked off.

"Andre doesn't like him," Leah whispered. "He's the son of a friend of ours." Leah had braided her hair wet the night before which gave her long, kinky curls. They looked terrific.

"I think he's sort of cute," said Robin.

"You would," said Erin. They all laughed.

"Does anybody know what we're supposed to be doing now?" asked Robin.

"I think we have to be checked by Kathy," Amy said.

That took about five minutes. "Now what?" asked Robin, heading for the food and coffee table which had been set up by the garage.

"Now we wait," said Leah, who had done a few commercials before.

"For how long?" asked Robin. She grabbed a couple of doughnut holes and a napkin.

Leah shook her head. "If I told you, you probably wouldn't believe me."

Leah wasn't kidding. By noon, they still hadn't done a thing, not even gotten into their positions. Cole, Keri, and Andrew were having fun chasing each other around the yard but the rest of them were bored, bored, bored. To pass the time, they'd interviewed Kathy, Kent, Mr. Fox, and a lady named Joanie who called herself the script girl. Her job was to make sure everything was timed right. The rest of the crew was too busy setting up to be interviewed right then.

Finally, they heard Marc calling to them to get into their positions. After they did, Kathy rushed around and patted their noses with powder and brushed their hair back. "Okay, ready," she said at last.

Marc went over their parts again, and they rehearsed a few more times with the music. "Now let's try it for real," he said.

Amy felt her heart start racing a little bit. This was it! Even without her glasses she could see that a crowd of spectators had gathered again.

Kathy did some more powder and then Marc said, "Take one. Action!" just like they do in the movies. Amy hung on to the rope ladder tight and pretended to sing her heart out.

"Cut!" yelled Marc, before they'd even finished the first verse. Something was wrong with one of the lights. They started over. "Take two. Action!"

Amy opened her mouth wide.

"Cut," said Marc. This time it looked like it was the camera. They waited about fifteen minutes. "Take three," Marc yelled.

Cole disappeared around the corner. "Cut," said Marc.

Janice brought Cole back, kicking and screaming. "I think he's ready for lunch."

Marc looked at his watch. "You're right," he said. "Break for one hour."

Amy, Leah, Erin, and Robin gathered by the kitchen door. "Is it always this way?" Amy asked.

"Always," said Leah.

Robin pointed at the food table. "Wow," she said. "Look what they're putting out for lunch. It looks like Thanksgiving!"

"One of the best parts of doing a commercial," said Leah in a knowledgeable voice, "is the food."

They all had a great time stuffing themselves. Even Leah, who normally didn't eat chocolate because she heard it gave you pimples, had all three of the desserts—brownies, chocolate mousse, and chocolate-chip cookies.

It took all afternoon to shoot the commercial. They must have done it fifty times, and they must have started over thirty more. By the time Marc said they were finished ("That's a wrap," is what he actually said), it was past five o'clock. By then, all of Amy's, Robin's, and Erin's families, plus about eighty other people, were standing around watching.

All Amy wanted to do was curl up in bed with a book, but instead Marc said, "Great job, everybody. What do you say I take you all out to dinner? Actors and crew."

"Yeah!" said Robin. From the treehouse window she shouted, "Hey, Ma, can I go out to dinner with these guys?"

Her mother nodded yes.

"I heard about a great new restaurant near here," Marc continued. "Have any of you tried Ondine's?"

Amy gulped.

"I hear it's fabulous," said Joanie.

"Roberta Rall gave it a bad review," said a guy named Tony.

"She gives everyone bad reviews," said Marc loudly. "Where does she think she is? New York?"

Amy glanced at Mr. Fox, who was smiling politely. No help there. "Kent," Marc was saying, "call them and see if you can get a six-thirty reservation. It'll take at least an hour to wrap things up here."

Amy looked at Erin, and Erin looked at Amy. "Say something," Erin hissed. "Tell them we can't go. Think what it'll look like if we show up."

Amy's face turned red. If Mr. Fox wasn't going to say anything, how could she? She couldn't be rude, especially under the circumstances.

Leah and Robin poked their heads through

the hatch. "Amy," Robin said under her breath, "do something!"

Erin said to Leah, "Why won't your father say anything?"

"He's being polite," said Leah. She moaned. "Just thinking about that place gives me indigestion."

"So does this mean we're going?" asked Robin.

Amy grimaced. "I guess it does. Maybe if we sit in a dark corner and squish down low Mr. Choux won't notice us."

Luckily, when they all arrived at Ondine's, the only person around was the man with the bow tie. Marc strolled over and said, "Good evening. We have a reservation for twenty for Goldstein."

The man looked at Marc. "I'm sorry, sir. Jacket and tie required."

Marc made a face. "Give me a break! I'm bringing twenty people for dinner."

"Sorry, sir, those are the rules," said the man.

Amy looked at Erin and then held her breath. Maybe they wouldn't have to eat at Ondine's after all. Maybe they would be spared.

Marc looked like he was getting mad. "You mean to tell me you'll turn down twenty people just because we don't have jackets and ties?"

"Yeah! Yeah!" whispered Erin. "Do it!"

The man sighed. "No, sir," he said. "If you wish, we have a few spares in the coatroom."

Erin groaned. "Darn!" she said.

While Marc and the rest of the men put on coats and ties, the ladies were led into the dining room. Amy kept her eyes riveted to the carpet. She, Erin, Robin, and Leah crowded together at the far end of the table.

"Would anyone care for a drink?" the waiter asked them. Over his jacket pocket the name "Pierre" was embroidered.

They all ordered Shirley Temples. Robin asked for extra cherries.

When Marc and the rest of the guys finally showed up, everyone had a good time making fun of their jackets and ties. "They must have gotten these from a rummage sale," Marc was saying. He had on a plaid polyester jacket and wide purple tie. Leah's father looked even more ridiculous. He had on a bright red jacket with a matching red tie. "I thought I'd try monochromatic," he said to Kathy with a wink.

At last, Pierre came over and took everyone's order. Amy ordered some sort of fish. She wasn't exactly sure how it was cooked, but Joanie, who spoke French, said she thought Amy would like it.

So far, they had seen no sign of Mr. Choux.

111

Amy started to relax. Maybe he was off tonight.

Then just as she started to bite into her fish, it happened. From inside the kitchen she heard an unmistakable voice saying, "Jacques! Pick up!"

Leah froze.

"That's him!" said Erin.

"Where?" said Robin.

"That's his voice we heard," said Amy.

From the other end of the table, Marc said, "How is everything, girls?"

"It looks delicious," said Amy. She took a bite of her fish and smiled at Marc. "Mmmm!"

Erin leaned over and whispered, "What do we do?"

"Eat," said Amy.

"I wasn't joking," said Erin.

"Neither was I," said Amy. "What else can we do?"

Robin had already dug in. "This steak is really good," she said.

"It looks overcooked," said Leah.

"I ordered it well done," said Robin.

Amy took another bite of her fish. "This is good, too," she said, surprised. "What did you get, Leah?"

Leah was poking her fork around in her food. "Veal piccata," she said. "This time I

112

brought Alka-Seltzer." She slowly chewed her first bite.

"How is it?" said Erin.

Leah took another bite. Next she sampled her vegetables. She glanced over at her father. "Good," she said. She took another bite. "Very good."

"Mine is really yummy," said Robin. "I don't see why you didn't like this place."

Erin gave her a kick under the table.

"Ow!"

"How's yours?" Amy asked Erin.

"Fine," said Erin. She'd ordered some sort of pasta dish.

The rest of the table was raving about the food, too. Even Mr. Fox.

Pierre came over. "And how is everything?" he asked.

"Delicious," said Marc. "Please tell the chef he did an excellent job."

Pierre bowed. "Monsieur, I'll do better than that. I will let you tell him in person!"

Amy practically choked, but before any of them had a chance to run and hide, Chef Choux appeared at their table.

"Your food is excellent," said Marc, smiling away. "We really enjoyed our meal."

"Ahh! I am so happy," said Mr. Choux. His eye suddenly caught Amy's. She slid a little lower in her chair.

Chef Choux steered himself down to their

113

end of the table. "So!" he said. He gave a big smile. "I see you decided to try me out again!"

"Um, er, well." Amy struggled for an answer. Wasn't he going to ask about the money? Wasn't he mad at them?

"Well, what did you think?"

"It was delicious," blurted Robin. "We all loved it."

Mr. Choux gave a happy grunt. "Good!" He turned to Leah. "Now about that pâté . . ."

"What about it?" said Leah cautiously.

"I think you were right. It was a bit dry that night." He called back to the kitchen. "Jacques, bring me one nice pâté, okay?"

Seconds later, Jacques whisked out of the kitchen carrying a small saucer. "Now try," said Mr. Choux, placing it in front of Leah.

Leah smiled weakly and took a small bite. Her face brightened. "It's good," she said. "Much better."

"You see!" said Chef Choux. "My new version. Even that crab apple woman from the newspaper liked it."

"She's too picky," said Marc. "This place is terrific." His jacket and tie made him look like an appliance salesman.

"I'm so glad," murmured Mr. Choux.

"Uh, Chef Choux," said Amy, "we have your money."

"What money?"

"The, uh, ad money," said Amy.

Mr. Choux waved his hand. "Forget about it."

Amy looked at Erin. "Are you sure?"

"Pffft," he said, looking away. "Sometimes even a chef slips up. Now we start over, yes?"

Amy grinned. "Yes," she said. "Maybe you'd even like to be reviewed again sometime."

"My *plaisir*," he answered. He signaled to Pierre. "Please bring over a plate of brownies for my friends here. I'm pleased to have them back as customers."

"And we," said Amy, letting out a deep breath, "are happy to be back!"

MEET THE GIRLS FROM CABIN SIX IN

Coming Soon
CAMP SUNNYSIDE #7
A WITCH IN CABIN SIX
75912-8 ($2.95 US/$3.50 Can)

CAMP SUNNYSIDE #6
KATIE STEALS THE SHOW
75910-1 ($2.95 US/$3.50 Can)

*Don't Miss These Other
Camp Sunnyside Adventures:*

(#5) LOOKING FOR TROUBLE
75909-8 ($2.50 US/$2.95 Can)

(#4) NEW GIRL IN CABIN SIX
75703-6 ($2.50 US/$2.95 Can)

(#3) COLOR WAR!
75702-8 ($2.50 US/$2.95 Can)

(#2) CABIN SIX PLAYS CUPID
75701-X ($2.50 US/$2.95 Can)

(#1) NO BOYS ALLOWED!
75700-1 ($2.50 US/$2.95 Can)